TH...
MOON ...

Also by Steven Kelly:

INVISIBLE ARCHITECTURE

THE
MOON RISING

STEVEN KELLY

An *Abacus* Book

First published in Great Britain in 1994 by Abacus

A CIP catalogue record for this book
is available from the British Library.

ISBN 0 349 10521 9

Typeset by M Rules
Printed and bound in Great Britain by
Clays Ltd, St Ives plc

Abacus
A Division of
Little, Brown and Company (UK) Limited
Brettenham House
Lancaster Place
London WC2 7EN

No one eats oranges
under the full moon.
One must eat fruit
which is green and cold.

LORCA

I opened the french windows and stepped through them. The wind was strong. It blew snow on to the balcony and past me into the room. I took off my jeans and T-shirt and threw them behind me on to the bed. Naked, I stepped forward to the edge of the balcony and gripped the iron railings firmly in my hands. The metal was cold and my flesh stuck to it. I felt nothing. Snowflakes landed on my hair and turned to water which ran down my face and dripped from my chin and the end of my nose. Snow settled on my shoulders which were cold. I turned my head and licked some snow from my skin. It tasted fresh and melted in my mouth. After a minute I prized my hands from the railing and went back inside. I left the balcony doors open and the wind blew in. I shivered and lit a cigarette. Then I poured a shot of whisky from the bottle by the bed into a glass tumbler. I drank it in one gulp and poured another.

I picked up the worry beads from the bedside table and held the tassel between the thumb and forefinger of my right hand and I swung the chain in front of my eyes. There are thirty-three beads. I counted them. Then I sat down on the

1

end of the bed. The beads were a present from Angelo. On the day I left the village Angelo gave them to me. 'From my friend Saledin,' Angelo said. 'He too was a soldier of sorts and with these it is possible to last through many hours of doing nothing. They concentrate the mind. How else do you think I could have done this job for so long? Take them. Ha, I remember when Saledin gave them to me. He saw me admiring them and he said take them. They are yours, he said. And I said to him, like a fool, but these are precious to you. What if I lose them? Lose them, he said. Are you telling me that you have so little respect for our friendship? Well, I took them, and I know he would have wanted you to take them now. There are thirty-three beads. The number is symbolic of something, but don't ask me what. Just bring them back with you. They have been a long way one way or another.'

I twirled the worry beads on my fingers for a while then put them down again and took another sip of whisky and threw the half-smoked cigarette out of the open french windows. I looked at the time. I still had time. There was half an hour before I had to go on duty and Angelo, in any case, would be late. For as long as I can remember my uncle has always been late for work. I smiled and lay back on the bed. The blanket felt warm under me and I shivered again. I reached out for the worry beads and placed them on my chest and played with them, tracing circles on my skin with the tassel. Then I threw them on to the floor in the corner of the room by the door and jumped up off the bed.

That is all I have. Worry beads and a few clothes. Nothing else in the room belongs to me. It is a typical hotel room. Bland, uniform, bare, though tasteful. I did own a lighter, but I gave that to a girl at the station in Bolzano. 'Do you have a light?' she asked me. Have a lighter, I said. It was a Zippo.

Army issue. Not something to keep. My sunglasses I gave to Elisa a long time ago. And everything else I threw out when I got back. Everything except the boots. And my father threw out all my other things while I was away. 'You are a man, now. You don't need that junk,' my father said to me. 'Yes, even your hi-fi. It was old and I'll buy you another. Yes, next month we'll go to Bolzano or even Milan. We could go to Milan and buy you some things. We'll get everything you need for your new room. You are a man, now. It's better this way. Believe me.' At first I was angry but now I do not care. In the army the thought of home, of my own things, it was important at times. But in the end it is the thoughts and not the things which count.

I crossed the room to the wardrobe and looked in the mirror. I thought I should shave, but I was not in the mood. There would be no one to see me, in any case. I looked closely at my reflection. My face has become heavier than it was before I left. That was the first thing Angelo said to me when he saw me. 'Your face is heavier, nephew. Some people would say that the face is only the surface, that it is weightless. But that doesn't cut any ice with me. The face gains weight with living. It suits you.'

Elisa did not think so. 'You're getting old before my eyes,' she said to me. 'And I'm getting old before your eyes. It's no good. I don't want to get old. I don't want to die.' I told her she was not going to die. 'You don't understand,' she said. 'I want never to die. I want to live for ever.'

Elisa was a hooker. On our first Friday night, with money in our pockets, we went to Number Sixty-Nine, the traditional first stop for new recruits. The madam looked at us closely. 'Your name?' 'Joachim.' 'You look like you need something to get a hold of. Room seven. You?' Andreas. 'Yes, I have just the thing for you. A nice girl for a nice young man. Room twenty-two. Special deal for first-timers like yourselves. An hour for the price of the usual twenty minutes. Make the most of it and don't forget to come back.'

When I went into the room Elisa was sitting in an armchair playing with an artist's mannequin, holding it by the head and moving its limbs into different positions. 'Hello, you are Andreas,' she said. 'And I am Elisa. The Duchess, she calls us to tell us your names. To make you feel more at home.' The Duchess? I asked her. 'Yes, her mother told her there was a one in three chance that Mussolini was her father. You can believe it if you want to. She's not a fascist at all, but a communist like the rest of Como. You'll learn that soon enough.' You are young. 'You call me young? What about

5

you. You are young. You are wet behind the ears. It's easy enough to see that from the way you're standing there. Are you going to stand there for ever? Come on, then. Clothes off. You might think an hour's a long time, but in an hour's time you'll think an hour is no time at all.'

It was against the rules, but I moved in with her. It was her idea. 'Of course,' she said. 'You should know that using a prostitute is just formal rape. You don't have to agree, but in any case I won't let you rape me any more. Just buy me flowers or books or something nice. The Duchess, she'll fix it with your officers. It's no problem. The Duchess can fix anything. And it's not as if you're a real soldier, anyway. You're just a cook who wears boots.'

The apartment was small but comfortable. 'The Duchess, my mother, she used to live here. That's why it's so nice. She gave it to me. I'm her favourite daughter.' It had a large balcony and Elisa draped old blankets and rugs over the railing so she could sunbathe naked on it without being watched. I liked her for her modesty, or for the incongruity of it. 'If people want me, they have to pay,' she said.

She liked me to cook for her. 'I get so bored of Italian food. It's nice to eat Austrian.' But I am Italian. I'm in the Italian army. How Italian can you get? She laughed: 'Ha, a lot more Italian than that. But they like your food.' They only tell you that because they like the fact that they're fucking my girlfriend. They like the way you fuck. 'Oh, poor Andreas, shacked up with a whore. What would your mama say?' My mama would never know. Being friends with Alexandra and her daughters is one thing, living with a full-time pro is another.

Elisa was right when she said her mother could fix things for me at the barracks. She also fixed it for me to work in the

6

officers' mess so I could be free all day when Elisa was not working. We would sleep together until late, eat lunch for breakfast, promenade together, make love again. Then I would go to my work and she would go to hers. It was a good arrangement. Soon the Duchess fixed things even better for me. 'I have your captain wrapped around my little finger,' she said. 'You leave him to me, Andreas. I'll take care of him and he will take care of you.' A few days later he called me back after parade. 'From tomorrow you just need to show your face in the right places once in a while. As a favour to the Duchess, you understand. And perhaps you can do me a favour too. Arrange it for me to visit Elisa now and again at her apartment. Once a week will be fine. I won't pay her, but perhaps I'll bring presents. There are all sorts of things I can get. You like hashish? Or opium? It's no problem.' From then on I went to the barracks every Friday to collect my pay and the rest of my time was my own. Elisa started working in the day, with weekends free. My captain would visit her once, maybe twice a week at our apartment – I would disappear for an hour – and the rest of the time we took life easy.'

'But if you married me,' she said, 'I could stop working. OK, perhaps I still see your captain because then it's better for you. But apart from that I would be yours.' I told her I did not care if she worked or not, why should I? 'You are a pimp,' she said. 'You want me to be with other guys. You are sick, yes, sick.' She slapped me on the cheek and left the apartment and did not come back for two days. Two days I spent alone in the apartment, not going out, not eating, not sleeping, not doing anything. When she came back I asked her where she had been. 'I have been reading a book by a great English writer called Cyril Connolly who is dead now. He said that according to some doctor, Charles Baudelaire was afraid to perfect his works because he was scared of the incest with his mother which would be his perfect fulfilment. Cyril Connolly says that perfectionists are notoriously lazy and that all true artistic indolence is deeply neurotic. That it's a pain, not a pleasure.' Then she took me to bed where we stayed for nearly a week. 'I'm on vacation,' she said.

I reached out and touched the mirror with my fingertips. I tapped the glass and then scratched a fingernail along the lettering in the top right-hand corner of the mirror. Hotel Weissman. It is etched in a frosty italic script. My uncle is always complaining about it. 'As if people don't know where they are,' he always says. 'In my opinion it is pretentious. To write the name of the hotel on every object whether it can be moved or not. I ask you, towels are one thing, but a telephone is another. Who's going to steal a telephone, after all? If you ask me, your father is an arsehole, but then he always was. You can't help him and that's the truth.'

It made me think of him when Elisa carefully printed her name in capitals on the inside cover of the first book I bought her. Elisa Borsatto. Why did you do that? I asked her. 'It's my name. Elisa Borsatto. Me.' I had not known what book to buy her so I asked her what she would like. 'The diaries of Cesare Pavese are very good and so sad.' She was disappointed when I gave her the book. 'But you hadn't even heard of him,' she said. 'You can't give me a book like this when you haven't even heard of him.' But you asked for it. You wanted it. 'No, no, I didn't. It is a wonderful book, yes, it is, but it means nothing to you. How can it mean anything to me if it means nothing to you? Buy me something else. Buy me something important to you.'

I thought about what she had said. It was only three or four days later that I had the courage to tell her: I can buy you nothing because there is nothing which is important to me. I am sorry. I just don't know how.

But Elisa loved books. She would take me to bookshops and we would spend hours browsing and at the end she would hand me a pile of paperbacks. 'Buy me these.' And once I did buy her flowers, but they made her sad. I gave her my sunglasses and she asked me if they were important to me. I squinted at her in the bright sunshine and said, Of course. I have blue eyes. That made her laugh. 'You are a very strange man, Andreas Weissman. Yes, you are. You are upside down and inside out and back to front. You have never learnt to do anything properly.'

I thought about that and decided that it was true. I knew I was supposed to buy Elisa flowers or perfume or chocolates. That I was supposed to feel jealous of the fact that she had sex with other men, especially when she said that she sometimes enjoyed it. I knew that I was supposed to miss my family and my friends in the village. But I did not know how. 'It's why I like you, so I shouldn't complain,' Elisa said. 'But it is very hard work at times. What it adds up to is that you don't know how to love me.' But I do love you, I said. 'Perhaps, but you don't know how to love me. It's different.'

Elisa. She was fascinated by names. She once discovered that Queen Dido of Carthage was known as Elissa. The spelling was close enough. She went immediately to the bookshop and bought a copy of Virgil and read me the story. 'But this I like,' she said. 'If you ever leave me, Andreas, be warned. This is what I shall do. I shall make a bonfire of everything you have touched and I shall jump into it and stab myself to death. Would you be sad if I did that, Andreas?' I will never leave you, I said. You are the one who will leave me. You will have a customer one day and that will be it, gone, just like that. 'But you are terrible. As if that's what I need. No, Andreas, you have me for ever, or my for ever, at least.'

But when I did tell her that I wanted to leave she did not burn herself or stab herself. And that made her sad as well. 'I should be Dido, Queen Dido of Carthage, and you should be my Aeneas. But we are nothing. This is nothing. You have taught me to feel nothing.'

I traced the outline of my reflection in the mirror. Elisa was a different type of person to me. That is how she would have put it. Sitting in a café, the waiter asks her what she would like. She reads the menu. She studies it. 'What brand of *espresso* do you use?' 'Splendid.' 'You have no Lavazza? Black?' 'It's possible. I can check.' 'Give me a *lungo*. Andreas, have you decided?' I'll have the same. 'On second thoughts, perhaps I should prefer an iced coffee. No, a lemon tea. Or an ice-cream. No, no, I'll have a *cappuccino* – or what time is it now? Oh, it's too late for a *cappuccino*. Give me an *espresso*. Preferably with Lavazza. No, a *lungo* after all. Yes, a *lungo* and Splendid will be fine.' Then she smiles, satisfied. She has made a decision.

Decisions, choices were so important to her. Opinion was everything. 'What do you think of this, or how about that? What do you mean? You are a cook, a chef, this is your speciality, how can you say that? Do you prefer my hair tied up, like this, or down like this?' I don't know. I don't mind. 'You are crazy, yes, crazy. Do you know what craziness is? I will tell you, yes, I shall. A crazy person is someone who won't identify with society. That's you. Normal people, people who aren't crazy like you, they can understand the world because they see themselves in it. They see the world in themselves. But you don't. You don't identify. You are a lunatic. Yes, that is the word for you. You should live on the moon because your mind is already there.'

I started to dress. I pulled on the trousers of my new suit, the new shirt, socks, boots, put on my tie and finally my new jacket. I took the jacket off again and laid it on the bed. Snow was settling on the carpet inside the balcony doors and the curtains were wet and flapping in the wind. I thought about closing the doors then I decided not to. Let part of this place belong to the mountains tonight, I thought. It's better that way. I sat on the bed and lit a cigarette and took a gulp of whisky from the glass.

Elisa used to love to watch me at work in the kitchen. 'I love it,' she would say. 'The way you take these things which used to be whole and you chop them up so they aren't whole any more and then you put them together again so they become whole again, but something else. It can't be done with everything. It's a special talent.' But I hate cooking. I have hated it ever since my father put me to work in the kitchens when I left school. 'If you won't study, you can do the work I tell you to do,' he told me. 'Then you will do your military service and after that it's up to you. You will be a man and you can make your own decisions.' In the kitchens

13

I started mopping the floors and carrying out the rubbish. Then I was promoted to washing dishes and after that they let me cut up onions and garlic. Small things become important. Sometimes onions have two centres and when their skin is peeled away they fall into two complete, though misshapen parts. I told Elisa about this once and showed her such an onion. 'The world is just a great big onion,' she said. And then she was sad for a few days and would not speak to me. Why are you sad, Elisa, I asked her. 'Is that how we are, Andreas? Like an onion with two centres but no skin, so only a little tug pulls us apart?'

In every moment of her life Elisa sought an image of herself in the world around her. She sought metaphor at every turn. If she saw a bird eating a worm she would ask me, 'Who is the bird, who is the worm? I don't mind being the worm because I should not like to eat worms myself, even if I were a bird. Will you be the bird, Andreas? Would you eat me? Your little worm? I shall wriggle for you if you do.' On New Year's Eve I took her to Vienna. We arrived at the Westbahnhof at eight in the morning. 'It is like the end of the world, all these fireworks,' she said. 'It is symbolic. I like it.' We drank beer for breakfast, checked into a hotel and slept for a while, took a taxi around the Gürtel because she wanted to know what Viennese hookers looked like. 'They are not so pretty. Not so pretty at all.' Dinner, then a bar, and Stephansplatz for midnight, champagne, kisses, a party on the trams and another in the hotel, more champagne. 'I did not enjoy tonight. The pizza was not made with mozzarella. If a pizza does not have mozzarella, it is not a true pizza. Take me home.'

I took off my boots again and lay back on the bed. I had time to kill. Last night I arrived on duty at eleven as I am supposed to and my uncle arrived an hour later. On the stroke of midnight. He came in, stamped snow from his feet, threw his anorak over the reception desk, searched his pockets for his tin of chewing tobacco, took a lump of tobacco, a wad, from the tin and slipped it inside his lower lip and then he looked at me with his eyes and mouth wide open. 'Ah, you are here,' he said. It is an old joke. When I was younger my uncle often took me into the mountains to walk in the meadows. We would arrange each expedition the day before, planning the route we would follow and what provisions we would need, and Angelo would always pretend to be surprised when I arrived at his room on time with my knapsack on my back, map and compass in hand. 'Ah, you are here,' he would say, sometimes emphasizing the 'you', sometimes the 'are', sometimes the 'here'.

And this will be my second night of work since my return, the second night of my new apprenticeship. My father asked me if I wanted to work in the kitchens and I said no, I would prefer to do something different. 'But we need a commis in

15

the kitchens. There are no other jobs for you. I don't know what to do with you.' It was Angelo's idea that I join him at night for a while. 'We can see, at least, if he has a taste for the work, though in my opinion you should give your son a holiday. Military service is no joke and a boy needs a rest when he's completed it.' My father looked at Angelo as if he were mad. 'Holiday? Yes, Andreas can have a holiday in a month or so, when the season is over and we all have our holidays. I do not make exceptions for my family. Andreas is a man now. He can take his holiday like the rest of us. Very well, you can learn Angelo's duties. Then there will be extra cover, at least, though I may be able to think of something better for you in the summer. Perhaps when old Hans retires we will need a new estate manager for the chalets. We will see.'

'Ah, you are here,' Angelo said last night. Then he came round to stand beside me behind the reception desk. 'On the wall over there,' he said. 'Behind the bar, you can see it, framed, these are some lines from Lorca, from his poem, "*La Luna Asoma.*" *Nadie comer naranjas bajo la luna llena. Es preciso comer fruta verde y helada.*' He stood looking at me, without speaking, for nearly half a minute before he went on. 'These are beautiful lines,' he said. 'And they remind me of the Alhambra palace where I worked for a season as a cleaner. We would arrive at nine, as the last visitors were leaving, collect our equipment and set to work. I cannot imagine eating an orange in that place. In the Casa Real an orange would be an obscenity. Olives. Green olives. Are they a fruit? Perhaps a poor excuse for a fruit and unripe with it. In any case, they are perfect for the Alhambra Palace. The perfect fruit to eat under the light of the full moon.'

Then he stopped talking and the two of us spent the rest of the night saying hardly a word to each other.

I felt uncomfortable. I wanted Angelo to ask me about my life

16

in Como, about what I had done in the military. I wanted to tell my uncle about Elisa, about my feelings now that I was back in the village, about what I wanted to do with myself. But every time I opened my mouth to speak, Angelo held up his hand and shook his head. Finally I accepted the silence between us. It seemed to me that Angelo was like an expert diamond cutter, contemplating the night as a stone he would cut, turning it over in his mind, examining it from every perspective, from within and without, seeking the lines of stress which would guide him in his first, decisive stroke. He would not be distracted.

The thought of that made me laugh. Elisa would have been proud to hear me. 'You are too literal for your own good,' she used to say to me. 'You have to learn metaphor, you have to learn to see the world a little more interestingly. I'm younger than you, but already I am bored of seeing the world as it is. You must live in a very boring world, Andreas Weissman, if all you see is reality and nothing else. Look, what do I have in my hand?' An empty beer bottle. 'No, no. This is my life. This is a poem. This is sex. This is love. This is your empty head. This is a garden. This is the stars and the moon and the sun and the sky. It is a worn-out hat which keeps your head warm, but doesn't keep it dry. It is everything you can think of.'

She would talk like that for hours. I would sit opposite her in a café, drinking beer or coffee while she articulated herself, her whole being, reinventing herself with every new thought, with every sentence she spoke. She would talk with passion. She would talk herself into a state of sexual excitement. 'Pay the bill,' she would say. And then, breathless and flushed, she would lead me by the hand back to her apartment and, without saying anything, we would make love as if for her it were the first time, as if through talking she had become a new person with a world to discover.

17

It was time. I pulled on my boots and tied the laces. I looked around my room and picked up my jacket from the bed, slung it over my shoulder. I left the light on and closed the door. The corridor was empty. I walked down the stairs instead of calling the lift. The lobby was quiet except for the receptionist. I do not remember her name, if I ever knew it.

'Good, you are on time,' she said and she smiled at me. 'You are much better than your uncle. I like it. This letter is for Angelo. Will you give it to him? Goodbye.'

When she had gone I sat at the reception desk. The chair was warm where the girl had been sitting. I loosened my tie and undid the top button of my shirt. It was quiet. I looked around the lobby, at the bar opposite, at the armchairs and coffee tables around the fireplace to the right of the bar, at the two telephone cabins in the middle of the lobby, at the dining area beyond them. The clock on the wall above the entrance clicked through a minute and I looked up at it. I was a little early but I had nothing better to do.

*

'On an aesthetic level,' Elisa said to me once, 'there is art on the one side and, on the other, philosophy and science. In terms of epistemology, you have intuition on one side and intellect on the other. With ethics there is freedom on one hand and security on the other – you can call that the individual versus social structure, if you prefer. And in terms of our ontology you can see voluntarism on the one side or determinism on the other. It's a neat system, don't you think? One of my clients was telling me about it while we had sex this afternoon. It was wonderful. I have discovered a new dialectic, he kept saying. Between the world of the soul and the world of logic. He was a very funny man and I liked him. For example: when you whisk cream to make it thick you are changing the form of the proteins which exist in the cream. You taught me this. And to know this itself is perhaps quite useful because it means that you know what you are doing. But, in fact, although you could measure exactly how long you need to whisk a particular type of cream with an electric blender, and this would be scientific, you do not do this. You do it by hand because you say it tastes better – and I think you are right – and you whisk it in such a way for as long as you think is needed or until it seems right and this is art or craft or whatever you want to call it. But the fact that you whisk it in the first place to achieve this result comes from empirical science, it comes from logical observation and application, so there is a dialectic at work between art and science and between intuition and intellect. Between logic and the soul. It's good, no?' For days afterwards she talked about nothing else. 'I am a hooker,' she would say. 'I don't like it much, but I want to know: if I stopped working at Number Sixty-Nine, would I still be a hooker or not? My mother was a hooker and so was my grandmother. Many women are hookers even if they do not think they are. I want to know:

is it in my nature to be a hooker, or can I choose to be something else? What do you think? And what about drugs? Of course, you could say that a society where drugs are illegal is better if less people are made unhappy by the drugs, but what if a law like this makes people even more unhappy than they would be, so they need the drugs even more, or think they do? What do you think of that? Aldous Huxley, who was a great English writer, he said that prohibiting alcohol as a way of curing the problem of alcohol abuse was like the surgical excision of pustules as a cure for smallpox. Well, we don't have smallpox in the world any more, but what do you think, in any case? I like the metaphor.'

After a while she grew tired of the subject. 'I don't like this any more. It makes me crazy thinking about everything in this way. Now I am my old self, I think. I will begin to live inside the dialectic again, so I don't have to think about it any more. It is more interesting that way. I will not see the philosopher any more. He can find another whore to fuck.'

I believe that Elisa never understood her ability to become someone new at a moment's notice. She once hinted at it. Reading Marcus Aurelius to me in bed one night, she laughed and in her laugh there was a hint of irony: ' "About what am I now employing my own soul? On every occasion I must ask myself this question, and inquire, what have I now in this part of me they call the ruling principle? and whose soul have I now? that of a child, or of a young man, or of a feeble woman, or of a tyrant, or of a domestic animal, or of a wild beast?" Shall I be a wild beast for you Andreas? Or would you prefer a pussy-cat tonight?'

I stood and walked around the reception area and the small office behind it where the security monitors showed some corridors of the hotel, all of them quiet and empty. Angelo did not teach me how to use the monitors last night, so I asked my brother to show me this afternoon. I flicked the switches and looked at every corridor in turn. There was nothing. Then I went across to the bar and poured myself a glass of whisky. 'If you drink anything you must write it in the book,' my father said when it was decided what job I would do. 'You will pay for any alcohol or extra food you eat from your salary at the end of the month. It is important to maintain good stock control. Even I pay for what I use. Manuel will show you where the book for the bar is, and the *maître* will show you the one for the kitchens. Do not forget. I had to fire a waiter, Marcello – you remember him – for theft, because he did not write down that he had a beer when he finished work. Please do not embarrass me.'

We seldom ate fish, but when we did, Elisa would stand in the kitchen with a copy of Jane Grigson's *Fish Cookery* in her

23

hand and read me the information about whichever fish we were to eat and the various recipes for cooking it. 'Red mullet. "Sometimes it is called Sea Woodcock, because of its liver which must on no account be discarded with the other innards. This delectable item was much prized by the Romans, who had a passion for red mullet. Martial exhorted his readers not to sully their gold platters with red mullet weighing less than two pounds. The Romans had a vulgar weakness for size." Ha, this woman. She is so English, it is painful. Her ass must be tighter than if someone stuck a cook's knife up it. But she's very good. We will have it *à la Bourguignonne*. With grapes.' There was a boy in the apartment next to ours. His mother was an alcoholic and left him there on his own. Whenever she wanted something done, Elisa would knock on the wall and a moment later he would appear. 'Go and buy us vine leaves, grapes, shallots. We have everything else.' And when we went out together for our afternoon stroll he would follow a short distance behind us, ready to carry Elisa's cardigan or to fan her if she was hot. 'My little dog,' she called him. But sometimes, when he was sad, he would run up to her and hold on to her waist and bury his face in her stomach. She would slap him lightly on the hand. 'Do not embarrass me,' she would say.

I went back to my seat and smoked a cigarette and a moment later, earlier than he was last night, my uncle arrived. He stamped his feet, threw his anorak over a chair and stood still for a moment. Then he went through his jacket pockets and took out his tin of chewing tobacco and put it on top of the reception desk. He took a wad of tobacco from the tin and put it inside his bottom lip and pushed it to one side with his tongue, put the lid back on the tin and looked at me with his eyes and mouth opened wide, as if he had not noticed me sitting there.

'Ah, you are here,' he said. Then he came round to stand beside my chair.

'On the wall over there,' he said. 'Behind the bar, you can see it, framed, these are some lines from Lorca, from his poem, *"La Luna Asoma." Nadie come naranjas bajo la luna llena. Es preciso comer fruta verde y helada.*'

He stood, nodding and looking at me without talking for nearly half a minute before he carried on.

'These are beautiful lines,' he said. 'And they remind me of the Alhambra Palace where I worked for a season as a cleaner. We would arrive at nine, as the last visitors were leaving, collect our equipment and set to work. I cannot imagine eating an orange in that place. In the Casa Real an orange would be an obscenity. Olives. Green olives. Are they a fruit? Perhaps a poor excuse for a fruit and unripe with it. In any case they are perfect for the Alhambra Palace, the perfect fruit to eat under the light of the full moon.'

For a moment I was struck by fear at the thought that we would again spend the night in silence, by the fear that my uncle intended through this lesson to show me the sense of routine which governs the job. But then Angelo continued, 'And that's what Manuel believes. By day he serves his Martinis after the classic model, with a twist of orange or lemon, but in the night he always puts in a green olive instead. Of course, then it's not a true Martini, but a Martinez which you are drinking; so Manuel insists at least. But sometimes poetry is more important than purism. You will learn that. Well, Lorca was a poet and in any case he is dead now. He can't be helped. We are here, we are now. We should not forget that.'

He sighed and glanced up as a guest came in and stamped

25

her feet on the mat inside the front door. She came over to us and Angelo waved a hand in the air and spoke to her. 'It is Manuel who put them there, these lines. He is an obsessive. You'll meet him tomorrow or perhaps you have already. He always does this, closes the bar and leaves me to serve the drinks while he goes to the brothel. He'll be back. If he's drunk he'll bring his whore with him. He's usually drunk. It is an occupational hazard with him, to be drunk and to smoke those filthy cigarettes of his. You know in Spain they cost nothing. Here they are expensive, but he pays for them. Through the nose; it's horrible. Well, perhaps for him it's an occupational hazard that he must visit the brothel three times each week. It would not be so important, but he has a wife and four children in Seville where he comes from and he spends half of his life here, two thousand kilometres away, or what do I know, and half of those nights with a prostitute. It's a joke. Manuel, he wants to save enough money to buy himself a bar. In Seville or maybe Marbella or Torremolinos. It's a joke. His whore gives him a discount, but still. He leaves at the end of the season with less money than he came with in the first place. There's nothing you can do for him even if the mood takes you. And then there's his wife. She's a good woman and passionate. She believes in breaking balls. Unfortunately, if I can't find Manuel at night, it's my balls she breaks. Wait. Listen. Seagulls. You hear them? We are two hundred kilometres or more from the sea. It's strange. Sometimes I wonder if God has played a trick on us. To hear seagulls when the sea is so far away, and on a night like this. Can you explain it?'

He shrugged and smiled and glanced at me and raised his eyebrows, as if to say that I should learn this lesson well. Then he handed the guest her room key and asked her, 'So, what do you think? The skiing, is it good? They say that the

skiing here is the best in Europe. I hope so for your sake. It
costs enough. I don't know, of course. I've never tried it. Can
you believe that? Born and brought up in these mountains
and I've never had skis on my feet in my life. It's a different
class of people who do this, who ski. In any case, was there
anything further?'

The woman tapped her key on the desk a couple of times
and asked for an alarm call in the morning.

'Aha, now. Did I show you this last night?' he asked me.
He pulled a ledger book down from the shelf behind him and
then took a pencil stub from behind his left ear. He frowned
when he looked at the tip and sharpened it a little with his
fingernail and licked it and then looked up at the woman
again. 'At eight, yes. And you would like coffee? Tea. OK.'
The tip of his tongue stuck out while he wrote and he read
each letter aloud. ' F-R-A-U-G-U-T-M-A-N.' Then he read
out what he had written. '8.00. Frau Gutman. 502. Tea.'

He took a piece of paper from a sheaf at the back of the
ledger. 'And now I write it again and later I will take this to
the kitchens for the breakfast waiters, so they know. Gaetano
or Luigi, I'm not sure, one of them will bring you tea.'

By the time he looked up again the woman was gone. He
put his pencil back behind his ear and gestured after her and
turned to me and jerked his thumb towards the staircase
where she had gone.

'Whore,' he said. 'They're all whores in this place. It
wouldn't be so bad but they think because they have money
they are special. Special whores, perhaps. Now, what's this?
Ah, from your father.'

He ripped open the grey envelope which I handed him.
Inside there was a sheet of hotel notepaper which he looked
at with his eyes screwed up. Then he nudged me out of the
way and searched through the desk drawers. He pulled out

his glasses, breathed on them and wiped them and then put them on.

'Motherfucker,' he said. 'He has a typewriter. Why doesn't he use it? His father was the same. That's doctors for you.' He crushed the note into a ball and threw it over his shoulder. 'What do I care for you and your fucking lists in any case?' he said. 'I fuck your wife's arse, that's what I care.' Then he took off his glasses and placed them on the desk before looking around the lobby. 'Time to bring the flags in,' he said. 'What sort of stupidity is it to have flags, anyway? What sort of a hotel needs flags?'

After a moment he pulled on his anorak and gloves and crossed the lobby to the main doors where he stopped to look out of the windows before he put his hood up and went outside.

I walked across to the windows but there was nothing to see. The snow was falling faster than it had been, the wind was stronger. It reminded me of Cortina where Elisa and I spent a week during the spring of our first year together. She loved to ski. 'The speed,' she would shout, 'I love the speed.' People would stare at her and she would call to them. 'Isn't the snow wonderful? It's so fresh. I want to take my clothes off and make love in the snow.' And they would turn away, confused. Towards the end of the week, though, she grew sad. 'I don't like it here. This is your home, the mountains. Not mine. I could never live with so much snow the whole time.' But there are mountains around Como. 'But not like these, not like this. Take me away. Take me home.'

Take me home. When she said it, whenever she said it, it was not the imperious command it might have been, but a lonely cry for help, frightened and bitter and sometimes a little anguished.

When Angelo came back inside he put the flags on the reception desk and started folding them and I folded one too. When we had finished folding the flags, Angelo said, 'In the morning it will be light when we knock off. If the weather is better I'll show you how the flags attach to the halyard. There's no point fumbling about in the dark. The clips are too small. You can't wear gloves. Your fingers get numb. You can't feel a thing. I'll show you in the morning.'

I did not say anything and Angelo put the flags away in their cupboard under the reception desk and then another guest came in. Angelo looked him up and down.

'You're lucky,' he said. 'In a few minutes I would have locked the door and my nephew and I would have gone on our rounds. I have to do them three times each night. They take twenty minutes if I hurry but tonight they would have taken twice that because I have to show Andreas where he must go and what his duties are. That's forty minutes you would have had to wait out there in the cold. And it is cold tonight, especially for the time of year. You can imagine how cold I get doing my rounds. Here in the main building it isn't so bad. There's heating. But in the car park and the chalet complex, there is no heating there. Well, I'll tell you a secret. On nights like this I don't bother. What's the point, I ask you? There's nothing to steal and no one comes here, in any case. Why should I waste my time walking the corridors of an empty hotel three times each night? It was different in the old days, but now? That's an hour every night. You can work it out for yourself, if you've a mind to. Two hundred and forty hours of every year walking around an empty hotel complex. There are better things to do with time than that. Well, you're lucky. Anyway, which room are you in?'

'I was wondering if I could get a drink,' the guest said. 'Is the bar still open?'

'Open, of course. That is a feature of the hotel. Twenty-four-hour bar. It's a pain in the arse if you ask me because I prefer a quiet life. At least if they paid someone to do the job at night I could sit quietly in my office, but you know what they're like. Well, it's not often that someone does want a drink and if I'm honest I can put up with the company. What will you have? Personally I don't like to drink these fancy cocktails. Manuel, he's the barman, he's always making these strange drinks. Well, some of them are OK if you like that sort of thing, but I ask you, whoever thought of putting a cherry in a glass of whisky?'

Angelo suddenly stopped speaking and took a step back and looked the guest up and down again. He was a young man wearing a suit and tie and he looked uncomfortable.

'Who are you?' Angelo asked him.

'Jim Nichol.'

Angelo reached out a hand and the guest took it and they shook.

'Mr Nichol,' said my uncle. 'Yes, I saw your name on the

register yesterday. Every night it's something I do. I like to know the names of our guests. I am Angelo and this is my nephew Andreas.'

They shook again and I stood and nodded to Nichol but I did not shake his hand. Nichol touched a finger to the side of his head and I did the same. My uncle said to him, 'But you are not Spanish.'

'No, but I work for Mr Thompson. In Malaga.'

'Ah, yes, this Mr Thompson. I have heard something about him. He is still out. I noticed because his key is still here and I have been told by one of the receptionists that I should look after Mr Thompson very well. Of course, if he's out I can't look after him at all. Where are you from? You are English I believe. There are many English people who come here. England, I used to work in England, you know, in London. In any case, what did you say you'll drink? I warn you, if it's a cocktail you want it'll have to be a Martini because they're the only ones I know how to make. And even then I prefer them without vermouth or this orange or lemon peel.'

'That sounds great,' said Nichol. 'I'll have some ice, though.'

'Ice, of course. You know, we use special ice here. It is taken from the glacier. I have not decided what my opinion is on the matter. In some ways it is appropriate. After all, we live in the mountains. It is winter. Yet we have refrigerators in every room. Can you explain that? On the other hand, to send a helicopter to the top of the mountain just to collect ice for people's drinks . . . At the very least it is pretentious. Come.'

He started towards the bar on the other side of the lobby, opposite the reception desk, and waved to Nichol to follow him.

'Sit.'

31

Then he went behind the bar and took two glasses from a shelf. He scooped some ice into them from a bucket and poured in large measures of gin. He handed a glass to Nichol and raised his own.

'Your health.'

'And yours.'

'Though to be honest it's a strange thing, to drink neat gin to someone's health. At best it is ironic. At worst, cynical. You only need to look at me to see that. And to tell the truth I've known a few drinkers in my life, good drinkers and good company if that's your taste in entertainment, to see a man so drunk he can barely talk and only then as if he has a whole onion in his mouth. Some places are better for it, of course. That's why I returned here in the end, you know. You can't spend your life washed up. And this isn't the sort of place where you can drink. Not really. In the winter it's too cold for that. For my taste, at least. In the summer, perhaps. Then I like to take a bottle of wine and some bread and cheese and apples into the meadows. In Paris we used to drink, though. If ever a city was made for drinking in, Paris is the one. There was nothing I liked more than to sit in the cafés with a glass or two of something, watching the world go by. The whores doing their business outside in the street, that was entertainment. And the police trying to catch them. You should have seen those bitches run, I can tell you. It would bring tears to my eyes, that and the gin they used to serve in those places. But it gives your drinking a certain expediency, to watch such things. Gives you something to do, at least. Tell me, when will your boss be back? I can't think where he is unless he has friends in the village. Will he be late? Perhaps I should light the fire if he's going to be late and you will be here long. No, really, it's no trouble. The manager, he doesn't allow me to light the fire at night, not unless there are guests. And to have a fire is good. In any case Andreas is here so it's no problem. You can tell your father, yes?'

I got up from my seat again and went over to the bar and pointed at the bottles of beer on the cold shelf. Angelo handed me a bottle and then took me by the arm and led me back to the desk.

'Andreas,' he said. 'Leave this to me. You want a beer, of course you can have a beer. Or a coffee or to sleep. Anything. It's no problem.'

He went across to the fireplace and raked it out and threw some firelighters on to the grate and some logs on top of them. It was soon burning quite well and as Angelo and Nichol were still at the bar I decided to sit next to the fire because it would be warmer and looking at it would give me something to do. Angelo did not say anything when he saw me go across the lobby and stood there behind the bar not talking while Nichol smoked a cigarette and drank his gin.

Elisa would play with fire. She would light a candle, even in the middle of the day, so she could play with the flame. She would wave her hand over it and through it, spill wax on to her skin and wait until it solidified when she would peel it off in long, thin strips. 'It's good,' she would say. 'Like peeling away your outside so it feels clean underneath. I like it.' Her mother, the Duchess, told me once that Elisa had a personality disorder. I could have told you that, I said. 'No, Andreas, I am serious now. When Elisa was a child she set fire to my bed, yes, it's true. Can you believe it. I was asleep, it was daytime, I had worked until late, and the next thing I knew my toes were alight. Oh, Andreas, it was such a shock. You be careful of my little Elisa. There's no point in taking her to a psychiatrist because they have no understanding of what it is like to be a whore's daughter, or a whore, for that fact. After all, they think everything is down to sex. But I know what Elisa needs, she just needs love. She'll be OK. Just keep on your toes if you're asleep, that's all.'

One of Elisa's clients, the first one I met, was a sculptor. He saw us in the street while we were taking our afternoon stroll. It was a Saturday or Sunday, I do not remember which. He came running up to us. 'You, you must be Andreas,' he said. 'Come, come to my studio and let's drink a coffee together.' Elisa had told me that she usually avoided seeing her clients away from Number Sixty-Nine but now she was curious. 'Yes, Andreas,' she said. 'Let's go. I'd like to see Rafael's place.' When we reached his studio in the Via C—, next door to Number Sixty-Nine, he made coffee and Elisa and I walked around looking at the sculptures which crowded the room.

'What I try to do,' he said, 'is incite desire. Desire. It is the most elusive of passions for the artist. There are many things a work of art can incite. Compassion, yes. Easy. Hatred, as well. Nausea comes without much trouble. Love has its problems but even love is not as tricky as desire. People know their desires better than they know what causes them to love. They can be fooled into loving, but they will never be tricked into desiring something they are repulsed by, never mind indifferent to.' His eyes gleamed as he spoke and Elisa and I smiled at each other. 'Yes, inciting desire. That is a challenge. To make someone forget that what they see is wood or stone or metal and to have them imagine, even only for an instant, that what they see or touch is a living creature, warm and inviting.' Elisa ran her hand down the back of one of the nudes. 'I think,' she said, 'that if I were blind . . . if it were a little softer and warmer . . .' 'Close your eyes,' said Rafael. 'Feel it.' He stood close to her and held her hands in his, guiding them over the surfaces of the wood. 'She is soft and warm,' he said quietly. 'Feel how soft and warm her skin is. Feel how the curves of her body guide your hands.' 'Yes,' said Elisa. 'Yes, she is real. Andreas, try this. You will see. She is real.' I sat on the corner of a table and smoked a cigarette while she went from sculpture to sculpture doing the same thing, exploring them with her hands and her face, gently resting her cheek against bronze breasts, stone thighs, wooden faces.

'But alas,' said Rafael. 'It is not enough. Andreas is not convinced. He is keeping his wits about him. And even I am not convinced. Perhaps while I am working on them, then I can imagine that my sculptures will become real, will come to life. Or again, in the night when they are just silhouettes or shadows, then sometimes they take me by surprise. Though never enough to make me want them. I am a perfectionist, it must be said. And it's perfectionism that inhibits me. Think about it. What is the urge to perfect your work if it isn't the urge to keep something of your own desires hidden, if it isn't the emblem of some secret guilt? And have you ever desired a woman who is perfect? This is my problem, Andreas. If I do not desire a woman, how can she be perfect? There must be some flaw which turns my loins to ice. But if I do desire a woman, that in itself is the flaw. How can she be perfect if she incites desire in a drunken old fool? This is the paradox.' He sighed deeply and stroked Elisa's hair. 'And of course,' he went on, 'I am tied to my models. I do what I can to avoid desiring them. Ask Elisa, she'll tell you. When I'm not working I visit her, what, twice a week? But when I am working, then it's three, four times a day. Just for the release of it, just to avoid desiring the model whose form I am using. That's another part of the problem. You exhaust yourself physically long before you exhaust your capacity to desire.'

35

Later Elisa and I sat on the balcony of our apartment drinking tea and eating chocolate cakes, listening to the dogs fighting in the street below and watching the old women on the roof terrace of the building opposite, hanging their washing out to dry and laughing and joking with each other as they worked. 'Rafael is crazy, but I like him,' she said. 'He is one of the few people I will allow to see me regularly. I can trust him not to fall in love with me. And he has the most wonderful hands. One day I will take a photograph of his hands and hang it on the wall.'

My uncle said, 'Of course it's true that the place to drink gin is Amsterdam. Have you been to Amsterdam? I knew a girl there once. It's an interesting story. I was travelling by rail from Vienna to Salzburg where there was a job for me if I wanted it. I was a young man. She was pretty. I didn't get off the train. Only when we reached Cologne did she ask me where I was going. I just smiled and she smiled back. She was a Jewess, a Survivor. Older than me, of course, which was part of the attraction. Six months we lived together in an apartment on the Warmoesstraat, next to a brothel, above the bar she owned. We would drink gin until we dropped. Every night, the same. At first I thought we were doing it for fun, then I tried to help her. How do you help someone who has seen what she had seen, though? It can't be done. So I just came to accept it. There are better things to do with your time, I suppose, than get drunk and share someone else's sorrow, but I didn't care. I was young. See, the fire is a good one. Good mountain wood, it burns brightly. It grows closer to the sun. That's what I like to think, anyway. Tell me, this Mr Thompson, what is his occupation?'

37

Nichol leaned forward and raised a hand as if he was about to say something but Angelo carried on talking: 'Of course, perhaps it is rude to ask these things. I am curious to a fault which is to do with the life I have led and naturally a matter of boredom. Can you imagine what this work is like? Don't ask me why I do it. I don't know. I have my fantasies, though. It's natural. When you spend seven hours each night staring into space your imagination comes awake. I have my dreams, daydreams like everyone has them. Just at night and with more time to consider them. And this place, it is a mysterious place, the hotel. No, I am serious. They say it is haunted. They say ghosts walk the corridors at night, keeping an eye on the place. Of course, I don't believe in ghosts and spectres. Who does? In the cold light of day it's easy enough to say that though. At night when you're on your own it's quite another thing.'

He knocked back his gin and filled up his glass again but Nichol covered his glass with a hand.

'Thanks, I'm fine for now. When Jonny – Mr Thompson – when he gets back I'll have some more.'

'Ah, yes, Mr Thompson. So, he must be at the brothel, I suppose. It's the only place he can be at this time of night if he doesn't have friends in the village. Have you been there as well? Though to call it a brothel is an exaggeration in my opinion. Their only regular customer is Manuel and he only ever visits Alexandra, the girls' mother. As for the girls, they are nice enough girls but at their age I can't imagine they know much about it. There's more to it than a pretty face and a skinny body. Young people don't understand that these days. My own nephews – not so much Andreas, but the other two – they are only interested in these Hollywood girls who come here. They never give the village girls a second glance. Me, I prefer them after the classical model. Good wide hips and a stomach. That's what's important. Manuel's whore, Alexandra, the girls' mother, she isn't bad for her age and she can be quite a charming woman when it suits her, though when she is charming you know she's after something. Are you married?'

Nichol did not answer at first, as if he was expecting Angelo to continue. Angelo stood with his shoulders back, his arms straight and his hands holding on to the edge of the bar and looked at Nichol without saying anything.

'No, I have a girlfriend,' Nichol said at last. 'One day we'll marry. There's no rush.'

'Good. If I'd thought you'd been at the brothel I might not have bothered serving you. To look at you it's enough to see that you're a decent enough man. That's not to say that decent people shouldn't go to the brothel if that's what they want. Why not? But they aren't right for everyone. Only a certain type of man can go to a brothel and come out decent at the end of it and if you don't mind my saying so you look like the type who'd need to keep his nose clean if he wanted to keep his shoes clean. This boss of yours, is he a good man? Ha, you're quiet. I had a friend, in Granada where I once worked for a while, he was a Muslim and he had many sayings. Intrigue, he would say if I was hiding something, intrigue is the work of Satan. Stop bullshitting me, he'd say.'

'Jonny's not a bad man. It depends what you mean by good.'

'Philosophers are thin on the ground these days, it's true. Saledin was a philosopher and an interesting man. He was Algerian and had some stories to tell, though when I knew him he'd stopped all that. He used to come to the Alhambra, where I worked. Every night he would come and sit in the Casa Real while we swept the floor around him. And when it was time for a break I'd sit with him and we'd smoke a quiet cigarette together and talk. He was a good man and could have answered your question for you. It's a crazy, mixed-up world we live in and I should know. I've lived in it. Most of the guests we get here haven't lived in the world. They might have travelled all over it but they haven't lived in it. Only the other day there was a man, a nice enough man, who was telling me that he's visited seventy-three countries and he sat where you're sitting now and listed every single one of them. Someone who had lived in the world instead of just visiting bits of it would have known better. I can tell you, there's nothing more boring than listening to a drunk German reciting a list of seventy-three countries.'

Nichol laughed and nodded and then the two of them did not say anything for a while. I just sat and drank my beer and stared at the fire.

One day we went to Lake Como to walk and eat a picnic. It was autumn. 'This wind,' she said. 'It makes me crazy. It makes me feel like I'm going to die.' She threw her arms around me. 'Hold me, Andreas. Hold me tight. I don't want to die, I don't want to die,' she would say. You're not going to die, I would answer. 'You don't understand,' she would say. 'I want never to die. I want to live for ever.'

This fear of hers was something which confused me but that day I thought I understood. Only someone who loved life as intensely as Elisa could fear death with such passion. Could find such pain within herself. I understand, I told her. She shook her head. 'No, no, you don't, you can't understand. You are content to be alive and to have nothing more. I don't want just to live. I want to live for ever. It's different. This wind, I don't mind it. I like it, really. It makes me feel as if I am on the edge of life. As if I am dying but not dying, living but not living. I don't know. How can I explain it in words.' She was thoughtful for a few minutes. Then: 'It's like with photographs. They are perfect things, photographs. They are so concrete but so delicate. If you look at them for too long they are not real any more. You stop believing in them. Or a kiss. It is only perfect for a few moments and then it is something else. Not a kiss any more but an exercise. I like your kisses because you know better than most men when to stop. Or look around us now, at this light. The light here will never again be exactly as we see it now. It is an instant and we cannot hold it. This is what a life is like and I am not content with it. I do not want my life to be a photograph or a kiss or a certain quality of light. It is just not good enough, it will not do for me. Raoul Vaneigem, who was a very great French writer, he thought that the orgasm is a glimpse of a transformed universe, that it offers the model of some perfect life for us. But he was not right. Orgasms are what they are because they end, and that is not enough.' I sighed and shook my head. You want more from life than is possible, I told her. 'Yes,' she said. 'Yes.'

Angelo walked over to the reception desk where he had left his keys and then went to the doors and locked them. While he was doing it the phone rang but I did not get up to answer it because my father had told me to leave it to my uncle unless he was away from the lobby. Angelo clapped his hands together and slapped his forehead.

'Can you believe it? At this time of night,' he said.

He went to the bar, took a big gulp of gin, and walked slowly over to the reception desk. He cleared his throat and picked up the receiver.

'Hotel Weissman. Yes, one moment. Mr Nichol, it is for you. I suppose you would prefer me to transfer it to a cabin, though I can't see the point because I have to go to the bathroom and Andreas won't listen to your conversation even if it is private. He's a good boy.'

Nichol took the receiver from him and cupped his hand over the mouthpiece until Angelo had left the room. I carried on watching the flames as if I had not even noticed the phone in the first place because I knew Nichol was looking at me and I did not feel like moving.

'Nichol. Yeah, sure. No, there's just me and the night porters. Yeah, two of them. No, I don't think so. What about the spic, is he still with you? Sorry. See you in a bit, then.'

He put the phone down and went back to his seat. He did not look at me but while he sipped his drink he stared around the lobby. He was sitting very still and I tried not to breathe because it had become so quiet. It seemed even quieter because there was someone else there. There was only the noise of the fire and the humming sound of the fridges behind the bar. Then the noise of my uncle on the stairs.

'Do you know, friend, this is a fucker of a job to have. To sit here alone with only the silence of the night for company. But it makes a philosopher of you, I'll say that. Andreas's father, my brother, the manager, he's an arsehole in most ways but I'll say one thing for him. There's no television down here. No radio. Just good classical music on that machine here. Shall I put some music on? Music is wonderful in the night. For myself I love choral music very much. *Carmina Burana*, it's wonderful. And Handel, a wonderful composer. But my favourite – shall I play some? My favourite is Mozart. Well, everyone loves Mozart these days and why not, but his music is wonderful. Ah, but I can see from your expression that you are not a fan . . .'

'No, no, whatever you like,' said Nichol. 'I'm a jazz man myself, but I'm happy with anything.'

'Some jazz we have, too. But in any case, music in the night is wonderful. Though now and again I like to sit here and listen to the mountains going about their business.' He laughed. 'Of course, I say I sit here alone with the silence of the night, but that's a joke. Silence? Listen.'

Angelo moved back behind the bar and they were quiet. The hum of the fridges and the fluorescents and the noise of the fire got louder. The wind made the windows shake. There was a creak from the floor above. Uncle Angelo whispered, 'Do you hear it?' and smiled and Nichol nodded and smiled as well.

'Silence?' asked Angelo quietly. 'Ha! You'd think two thousand metres up in the mountains in the middle of the night you'd get a bit of peace. But it doesn't work that way. There's always something going on. And as I say, it's a fucker of a job to have when you sit here alone all night with nothing but your thoughts for company.'

He sighed and leaned over the bar a little to stare into his empty glass from above and then looked at Nichol's glass and back again. Then he slapped the top of the bar and grabbed the gin bottle and poured them each another drink before Nichol had a chance to say no. Then he said, 'So, tell me, what do you do for this Mr Thompson? He is some kind of businessman, I believe. What is his trade?'

'I'm his personal assistant,' said Nichol.

'Yes, I see. Did I tell you that I worked in the Alhambra Palace for a season, as a cleaner? My friend, Saledin, who was a lecturer at the University of Granada, he was an expert on Moorish Spain. An intellectual. It is strange: although I am not an intellectual, I have gravitated towards them all my life. I cannot explain why. Saledin, yes, he had some interesting ideas about the Alhambra and its architects. He believed the building, beautiful as it is, to be a blasphemy against God, the work of heretics. They are surely in hell, now, he would say. He wrote a book about it, published in Cairo some years ago. I couldn't read it of course. Although I can speak a little of nine languages, Arabic is not one of them. It is very sad. One day I shall learn Arabic because they say it is the only way to read the Koran and truly, the Koran is a wondrful book. So, Saledin's book was called *Earthly Paradise*. This is ironic, he told me. Paradise on earth cannot be, but they thought it could. By "they" he meant the architects of the Alhambra. As he saw it, God brought forth form from formlessness to create the world. But to create such a building as the Casa Real, to create such beauty, Saledin believed, was to seek to emulate God or maybe even to become God in which case, perhaps, you need God no more. Well, for a religious man I can see that there might be a problem. Tell me, have you ever been to the Alhambra?'

Nichol took a cigarette from his packet and tapped it on the bar and lit it before he answered. The way he lit it made me want one as well so I went over to the machine and used my keys to get a new packet. There was only MS left but I did not mind and when I had opened the packet I lit a cigarette with a piece of wood from the fire. Nichol answered my uncle.

'Sure, now and again. Whenever Jonny has business in Granada we stay at the Parador there. Nice place.'

'Nice, yes, it is nice. It is beautiful. It is art. I only wish Saledin was here so we could discuss it but he's dead now. Manuel is an artist after his own fashion. He takes these cocktails of his seriously. No doubt he'll tell you something about them later if he comes. Whether he'll return or not I cannot say. He's a law to himself that way which is how a person should be. That's the Spanish for you, I suppose, with their hot blood. Not like us in the mountains which is something that has always fascinated me. But look, these books. Some of them are better than others I believe. This one is his favourite. By "Bernard". It's an interesting book. Look.'

He held the small, green hardback under Nichol's nose and dropped it on to the bar. Nichol's back went stiff but he picked the book up and started to flick through the pages while Angelo joined me by the fire and started to poke at it with a block of wood. Then he sat down next to me and took my hand in his own.

'Are you well, Andreas?' he asked me and I nodded. 'Good. You just shout if you need anything. You just tell me. Later we'll have a chat and some food, when Mr Nichol and his boss have gone to bed. We'll have some hot food tonight. It's better with this weather, a hot meal. I've seen it as bad. Worse, one time. When you were very young, though you shouldn't say things like that until the storm's blown over. Who can tell, after all? Did you hear the forecast? They predicted sunshine and no wind, but I spoke to Karl earlier. He was buying groceries, for a week, he said. He should know if anyone should. I just hope there's no one out there tonight, no one stupid enough to listen to weather forecasts.'

He spat his wad of tobacco into the fire and it fizzled and burnt. Then he went over to the reception desk and searched through his anorak and pulled out a cigarette packet. He shook it and squeezed it and then slipped a finger inside and slit open the top. He scratched his head and ran his fingers through his hair.

'Shit,' he said, and then he walked back over to the bar. He grabbed the cocktail book from Nichol's hands, turned some pages and started to read from it while he went round to the other side of the bar.

'The writer of this book has, for many years, made a habit of jotting down the recipe of every cocktail, that he has come across, which possessed special merit. The present compilation of well over a hundred recipes is the result of his notes. As he has travelled in various parts of the world and has gathered recipes from far and wide, the collection is more or less unique. Is that not wonderful? And look, the title of this book is *One Hundred Cocktails, How to Mix Them*. Yet there are well over a hundred recipes. It is as if the book is bursting with them. They say OK, we'll have a hundred

47

cocktails, but this man, Bernard, he can't find only a hundred recipes, so he puts in more. Now he was a true artist, Bernard. And this I like as well, his introduction. How the dictionaries define a cocktail, I do not know . . . This is wonderful. Bernard, he doesn't give a monkey's turd about dictionaries. He doesn't care how they define cocktails: but were I asked, he says, I should say that it was a delicate combination of ingredients, all of which contribute their share in building up a unique beverage, possessing an individualism of its own. This is poetry. But there's more: Whether the reader agrees with me or not hardly matters. What does matter is that he should appreciate that the ingredients of a cocktail have been thought out and selected by a master-mind who has blended them together to obtain a definite flavour. Thus to alter them, in substance or quantity, will surely alter the resulting effect – and, generally, an alteration means an inferior result.'

Angelo shut the book and threw it down on the bar surface and then looked at Nichol closely. Nichol coughed and looked away. Angelo jabbed his finger in the air and said, 'This man is an artist.' Then he laughed. 'Take it, read it yourself. See what you think. Manuel, if he comes, he'll talk about Bernard all night if he gets the chance. As I say, Manuel, he's an artist. He appreciates this book. He knows how to, because of the drinks. Me, I just like the way Bernard says things. I get more pleasure out of reading this than I do from drinking the cocktails which says something about words. Is that not a wonderful name for a cocktail barman? Bernard. You can imagine it. You go into a smart cocktail bar, an American bar, you start talking with the barman and you ask him his name and it's Bernard. Like the dogs with their brandy. Saint Bernard, the cocktail barman. Wonderful.'

While Nichol read the book Angelo looked at the CD jukebox at the end of the bar. He took the key from the top of the machine and opened the front, then pressed a switch a few times and closed the machine again and chose some music which I did not recognize. Nichol looked up when it started and asked Angelo what it was.

'Verdi,' said Angelo. '*Don Carlos.* "She doesn't love me . . ."' My uncle laughed loudly. 'Well, it's the story of my life and probably of everyone else's and the words have been said enough in most languages. It can't be helped.'

Nichol shrugged and went back to his reading and my uncle leaned an elbow on the bar and his chin on one hand while he played with his glass with the other. They stayed silent for a long time, hardly moving.

'Is your Hotel Weissman near to Davos?' Elisa asked me. I told her it was quite near. 'I think this is funny. I like this. I shall read Thomas Mann, *The Magic Mountain.* Then I will know how it is in your village.' She read the entire book in under a week. She hardly spoke to me during the whole time. Then she came running out on to the balcony where I was sitting in the sun not doing anything. 'But this is perfect,' she said. 'This line is perfect: "Your tale is told. We have told it to the end, and it was neither short nor long, but hermetic." I like this very much. This line makes this whole shitty book worth reading. You know, if everyone knew this line and knew how terrible this book was, they would not read it in the first place because they would already know the only good bit. But I am happy now.' And do you think you know what my village is like? 'Oh, no, but I have found out something about myself. I have discovered that I want to be hermetic. Will you be hermetic with me? Andreas, please say yes.'

There was laughter outside and then the sound of a key in the lock and the main doors swung open and banged against the doorstops. Manuel came in and Hanna's mother, Alexandra, came in behind him. She was giggling and dabbing her eyes with a lace-trimmed handkerchief. She blew me a kiss when she saw me sitting by the fire and I waved to them both and Manuel waved back to me before going over to the bar. He brushed the snow from his coat, then slapped Nichol on the back.

'Jim, I'd like you to meet my very good friend Alexandra. Alexandra, this is Jim. I was showing him how to make White Ladies at Mario's earlier, before I brought Jonny and Dave to see you.'

Alexandra tried to stop laughing and held her breath for a moment before she joined them and sat on a bar stool next to Nichol. Manuel snapped his fingers twice and said to Angelo, 'Hey, mate, who's on duty?'

Angelo screwed up his eyes before he answered.

'That depends on what you would like to drink.'

Manuel stretched and yawned and said, 'So, outta my way.'

Angelo moved to the end of the bar and let Manuel take his place.

'OK,' said Manuel. 'So we gonna have cocktails all round. Jim, you wanna cocktail? Alex, you get a Top Notch like usual. Jim, how about a Sidecar? You'll like a Sidecar. Sidecars are great. Hey, you've got Bernie. Look up Sidecar. Bernie's recipes are the best. Read it out to me, read it out.'

Manuel started setting up equipment on the bar surface while Nichol looked through the book for the recipe. He found it and started reading.

'Sidecar Cocktail. A quarter gill of brandy, eighth of a gill of dry gin, the juice of a quarter lemon, half a shakerful of broken ice –'

He stopped and looked up but Manuel told him to go on.

'Half-fill the shaker with broken ice and squeeze in the juice of quarter of a lemon. Then add the brandy and the dry gin. Shake well and pass through a strainer into a cocktail glass. This is a great favourite with the French and is fairly strong.'

Just as he finished speaking, Manuel put a glass down in front of him and poured the drink into it.

'Bernie's the best,' he said. 'I'm telling you. Now, Alex, your turn. Read it out, Top Notch.'

Alexandra found the page and started reading quickly, without breathing even once.

'One teaspoonful of raspberry syrup a quarter of French vermouth a quarter gill of sloe gin a cherry half a tumblerful of broken ice half fill a tumbler with broken ice then put in the French vermouth the sloe gin and the raspberry syrup stir well and pass through a strainer into a cocktail glass and serve with a cherry . . .'

She stopped and picked up her glass while Manuel put a cherry on to a cocktail stick, let him add the cherry, sipped the drink and nodded and finished reading. 'This is a sweet cocktail and is very popular among the fair sex. One day I'm going to win, I'm going to beat you. You know, Jim, Manuel, he does this with everyone, even with the guests, yes, and he tells them that if they finish reading the recipe before he finishes making the drink they can have it and the next one free. It's very stupid, I think, but I like it.'

Manuel grinned and started mixing his own drink more slowly and Nichol stirred his cocktail with his finger which he licked. Then Nichol said, 'Is Mr Thompson – Jonny – is he coming or is he going to stay there all night?'

Alexandra shrugged and raised her hands palms-upward. 'The girls, they are young. They have a lot of energy. I think he will come soon. With Hanna, perhaps.'

Manuel opened the jukebox. He cancelled the music and made another selection.

'This is better,' he said. 'Hot jazz for a cold night. Come on, let's sit by the fire.'

The others followed him over and they sat down in the chairs next to me. Alexandra gave me a quick hug and kissed my cheek and asked me if I wanted a drink but I said that I was OK and I would get another beer in a minute.

'Would you look at that snow,' Angelo said in a loud voice. 'Nearly April already and it's snowing like this. Of course, it often snows at this time of year, but like this? It reminds me of Eliot. April is the cruellest month. Normally you'd disagree but, for once, perhaps he had a point. He visited the village one time, you know. T. S. Eliot. His name is in the visitor's book. That was a long time ago. Many poets and artists used to visit here. Because so many of their friends stayed in the sanatorium while they died. Now we just get pop stars who don't know the meaning of the word. April. Are you aware that tonight we must put the clocks forward by one hour? Yes, at one o'clock. At one o'clock it will be two o'clock. I have seen this many times, of course, but you never get used to it. And I can remember some times when it has caused trouble. In London, once, when I was working in a nightclub in the centre of the town, in the West End. Normally we closed the place at two and, of course, because one became two, many of the customers were very upset to find that although they had paid their money they would have to leave one hour earlier than they expected. There was a fight and the whole place was wrecked before the police came. In some ways you can see the funny side, but at the time it was frightening, to see such anger and violence. It's a strange thing. To live in a world where we do everything by the clock except twice a year when we all agree to ignore the old rules and follow the new ones. It is as if something has slipped.' He snapped his fingers. 'Just like that. I recall in Madrid when I was visiting, there was a man who we would often see in the street. When he walked he was very careful to put one foot precisely in front of the other, as if he was on a tightrope. When someone walked too close to him he would stop walking and stand still as stone until they had passed. I don't know what went on in his mind, but they told me that he believed he was walking on the very edge of the world, and that unless he was careful he would fall off. That is how it is, sometimes, when you think about time.'

None of the others answered and after a few minutes Alexandra whispered something in Manuel's ear and the two of them got up. Alexandra waited by the lift while Manuel checked the register and took a room key. He told Angelo the number and then joined Alexandra. They went into the lift when it came. The doors closed behind them and it started up and we three were left sitting in silence by the fire. I threw a log on to the fire because I wanted it to be hotter but my uncle got up straight away and took if off again because he was worried that the chimney might be set alight.

'Young Andreas here has recently completed his military service,' said Angelo. 'You do not have such a thing in England I believe.'

Nichol looked at me with interest. 'No, but I was in the army, the Paras. What about you?'

I told him that I had been a cook and he laughed.

'Well, someone's got to do it, I suppose. And some of the best men I knew were in catering. Wild bunch of lads. You must have had a party or two.'

I nodded but said nothing. In fact I only went on to base once in the last six months I served, when I returned my uniform and my rifle. No one had missed me; most of the people I had started with had already left. My captain took me for a drink and congratulated me. 'I am always proud when a member of my company succeeds in escaping duty as much as you have, even if you did have some help from me. Well done. And how is Elisa? Give her my regards. And her mother as well, though I shall be seeing her tonight, I hope.' He did not ask me what I would be doing now that my service was over. I did not tell him that I had said goodbye to Elisa, that I would never see the Duchess again.

fter a while I decided to make myself a coffee and I asked my uncle and Nichol if they wanted one, but they did not. I had to go to the kitchens to make it because the espresso machine behind the bar had been out of order all day.

While I was waiting for the coffee I smoked another cigarette and walked around the kitchens to see if any food had been left out. We would eat later but I was quite hungry. There was nothing so I drank the coffee strong and black but without sugar because it would stop me from feeling so hungry and also because it would help keep me awake and I was getting tired. I could have gone to bed anytime because my father told Angelo not to let me get too tired in my first week, but I wanted to see if Hanna would come because I had not seen her since I got back. Anyway, if I was going to do this job, it was better if I got used to staying up as soon as possible.

One afternoon I was taking a siesta in the sitting-room and I awoke to find myself staring into Rafael's eyes. He was leaning over me, his face only inches from mine. For a moment neither of us moved, then he jumped back. 'But it is incredible,' he said. 'Elisa, he is always like this when he sleeps? So like a statue. Forgive me, Andreas, I have been studying you for ten minutes, I did not mean to wake you. But not even your eyes move when you sleep. Do you not dream? And your breathing, it is so shallow. With that pale Northern skin of yours, it's as if you are dead lying there. It's astonishing. Elisa, bring your lover a beer and one for me, as well. Come on, let's sit outside. The sun is on your balcony still and it's a warm day for the time of year. It's an Indian summer.'

I went to the bathroom and washed my face and then joined Rafael and Elisa. She was sitting, naked, on the floor of the balcony and Rafael was sketching her. 'An experiment, Andreas,' he said. 'I have never used Elisa as a model, only as a counterpoint in my work. But recently one of my models seduced me. I could do nothing to stop it happening, so I decided to try things a different way round. We'll see what happens.' I looked over his shoulder at the sketches. They were simple outlines with no shadow to show depth and Rafael did not draw Elisa's head or hands or feet. 'She's no Venus. Too skinny for that. Usually I like them with a few bumps here and there. Your girlfriend is just a child. It's interesting for me.'

I sat back and watched as Rafael directed Elisa into different positions. Sometimes she smiled at me, but mostly she concentrated on following Rafael's instructions. 'What material will you use?' she asked him. 'Oh, wood I should think. For me, wood is the most difficult, but it is warmer. I prefer to use it with my younger models.' 'And if you sculpted Andreas, then, what material would you use then?' Rafael turned to look at me and smiled slightly. 'For

Andreas, nothing less than spun silver would do. Platinum, if I could get it. Don't tempt me. I'm a poor man.' 'Silver,' said Elisa. 'Yes, that is right. The colour of the moon.' She threw her head back, arching her neck and spine as she stretched slowly. 'I'm getting cold now. Enough.'

When I got back to the lobby Nichol had fallen asleep, and even when the doorbell rang and Angelo's bleeper went off at the same time he did not wake up. Angelo ignored the doorbell at first and switched his bleeper off, but then he sighed.

'Fuck them and their doorbell at quarter to one in the morning,' he said.

He stood up and slowly crossed the lobby and opened the door. I recognized Thompson because I had seen him around in the lobby earlier in the evening. He had been drinking on his own at the bar and when I passed him he shouted to me: 'You, do you fancy helping me get pissed this evening?' I had just looked at him and gone on my way.

He seemed quite drunk now because his face was red, though it may have been the cold. He threw the umbrella he was carrying down on the floor, pushed past Angelo and walked straight to the bar and thumped the surface.

'What do you got to do to get a bloody drink in this place?' he said. 'Where's that dozy sod Manuel?'

He was followed in by another man who joined him at the

61

bar after nodding to Angelo. Hanna stayed in the doorway for a moment, then smiled at my uncle and squeezed his shoulder. Then she joined the other two at the bar.

Thompson took off his overcoat and looked around for somewhere to put it. He did not seem to see the pegs by the reception desk and folded it and put it on the floor by the bar.

'Davy,' he said. 'Wake that bastard up and then you can shoot back down to the village before this bloody snow gets any worse.'

Davy scraped off some of the snow which had settled on the shoulders of his coat and came across to the fireplace and slipped the snow inside the collar of Nichol's shirt. Nichol woke up straight away and shouted, 'You fucking artist, Davy. What did you go and do that for?'

'I'm heading back down to Alexandra's place, all right? See you in the morning.'

Then he saluted Thompson and Hanna and picked the umbrella up and went. Angelo locked the door behind him and turned to face Thompson who was standing with his back to the bar pointing at him.

'You.' He jabbed the air. 'Are you going to fix me a drink or do I have to do it myself?'

My uncle went behind the bar and bowed to Thompson. 'Please.'

'OK,' said Thompson. 'Three beers. Do you want a beer, Hanna? And one for yourself, barman. Whatever you want.'

Nichol went over and sat on the other side of Thompson from Hanna, rubbed his eyes and yawned.

'So where's Manuel and Alexandra?' Thompson asked him. 'He promised me he'd mix us up some more of those cocktails he was going on about earlier. Where the fuck is he, then?'

'The two of them went upstairs a while ago, just five minutes ago. They'll be back. How are things?'

'All right.' He sniffed. 'Yeah, not bad at all. Doesn't Hanna look resplendent? Stand up, Hanna, show him what you're made of. What do you think of that? Beautiful, that is. Bloody lovely.'

Nichol nodded and looked Hanna up and down and she smiled and twirled and sat down again. She had grown up a lot since I had last seen her and she looked quite pretty. Angelo put three beers on to the bar top and opened them. Then he filled his own glass with the last of the open gin bottle and threw the empty bottle into the bin behind the bar and there was the clink and crash of glass breaking.

'Cheers,' said Thompson.

'Cheers. So Davy's having a good time, then.'

'Could say that. He's only in there with bloody two of them, now. Hanna's sisters. You didn't meet them either. They're twins. Good girls. I tell you, he can't believe it. Tell you what, though, if his bird finds out about it he won't be shafting anything for a while.'

'Yeah, well, that ought to keep him in line for a bit. Have you called in tonight?'

'No, the boys are in Granada this evening. They've got a meeting with Yusuf. I'll call them a bit later. Keep them on their toes.'

Angelo interrupted. 'Granada? It is a wonderful city. You know it well, Mr Thompson? Mr Nichol has told me that you sometimes visit Granada and stay at the Parador San Francisco. Sometimes, in the evenings, we used to go there to drink *sangría* and talk before we started work. On the patio, behind it, you know this place. It is wonderful to sit there in the evenings. But tell me, what is the purpose of your visit here? I know you have not skied because I did not see you this morning when the party gathered. Not that they got much skiing done, mind you. Are you here for business? Or just for the air. The mountain air is very fresh. In former times there was a sanatorium on this site, for consumptives. That's not to say you are a consumptive – of course not – but still, people come here for their health.'

Thompson laughed. 'Yeah, I guess you could say I'm here for my health. No, I just thought I'd take a little holiday. Get away from it all for a while. We've been all over. Up through Madrid and Barcelona, along the south coast of France and up along here. It's been a very pleasant trip, as a matter of fact. And profitable. Some people don't believe in mixing business with pleasure, but I do. I had a meeting in Milan on Thursday and I've got another in Venice tomorrow. Then I'm laughing all the way to my bank in Berne. That's what I call mixing business with pleasure.'

'Yes, I can imagine. I can see that you are a businessman. What do you do in Malaga?'

'Import-Export. Here's my card. Keep it.'

Angelo held the card close to his eyes and studied it.

'"Thompson's Import-Export Agency",' he said. 'Yes, this is impressive. And very interesting. For myself I have never been tempted by the business life. I prefer it this way, to work in simple jobs and earn enough to keep me content. What else do you need? Well, if you have to work at all, I suppose. Of course, it would be better never to have to work and not at all boring, but still.'

'Yeah, well, that's life isn't it. If you don't work you don't eat, do you. It stands to reason.'

'That's life, yes. A banality, but still, it is life even if it is banal. Take, for example, this work of mine. What has it got to do with eating? Why do I do this job in particular? Once upon a time there was a point to it, when you had to watch over the patients at night and fetch the doctor if one of them was sick or dead or something. But now, here, in this hotel?

64

It is a stupidity.'

'Come on, mate. The fact that you're here means people can sleep safely in their beds at night, that's why. Not to mention get a drink, which counts for enough in my book. I'm sure you're very much appreciated.'

'No, no, you do not need to say this. What I mean is that if everyone was honest then my job would have no purpose in any case. Also, however, there are five hotels in the village and only this one has a night porter. And now it has two.' He waved his hand in my direction and Thompson turned to look. I bent my head so that he would not see that I had been watching. 'So this hotel is very much more expensive by the amount it costs to pay me and my nephew and give us our rooms and food because, you know, even though we are family, we must be paid.'

'Your family owns this place?' Thompson sounded quite surprised.

'Of course,' said Angelo. 'This is Hotel Weissman and that's me, Weissman. Anyhow, it is all a question of profit. But profit is not used to buy food. And there is much profit, all of it just spent to make more profit which, in turn, will be spent to make even more profit. It's obvious: it is absurd. How can it go on, tell me that. Where does it all end? There is only so much of the world, after all. It has to end somewhere. In any case, perhaps there are more interesting topics for us to discuss. Tell me, how long have you lived in Spain? Do you like it there? I have had many adventures in Spain. I remember when I visited friends in Segovia, in the province, some years ago. We went to a fiesta in a small village. It was very exciting. There was a girl, of course. Always the most exciting moments in my life have involved a girl. It's only natural, you could say, with the way men are and I am sure you're the same yourself. Justina was her name and she was very beautiful. Tall, taller than me, and dark-haired with that olive-coloured skin they all have down there. Legs which went on for ever and such an arse it would make you cry. A typical Spanish girl in many respects. That was an adventure, I can tell you. My good friend Eduardo, who is from Segovia, and some other friends who came with us. We arrived in this village on the first day of the fiesta. I must be careful in the sun and it was very hot, even in September it was nearly forty degrees in the shade. You can imagine it, I'm sure. We went straight to a bar, of course, to drink a beer. Justina was there and I noticed that she was staring at me. Well, to tell the truth I am used to the stares of strangers. It's something you have to live with and it has its benefits. So, the fact that she was staring didn't interest me much. There were better things to think about, like, for example, trying to understand the language, because I didn't speak Spanish in those days. And I was drinking my beer. I noticed an insect on the arm of my chair, just a normal, little black insect with wings. And I killed it by wiping my beer bottle over it, crunching it into a little black ball which the next draught carried away into the sawdust on the floor. It was nothing. You'd do it every day yourself. The minds of Spanish women are strange, I can tell you. Not a minute later Justina was sitting beside me. I saw how you killed that insect, she said. Immediately I could see that you are a real man. Meet me here at midnight. Then she left to watch the bullfight from the balcony of her grand-father's house on the square.'

He stopped talking, and Thompson looked at Nichol with one eyebrow raised. Then Nichol asked. 'And did she meet you?'

'Of course. At midnight we met as she had said and we danced in the sand of the bull-ring where they had set up a disco, we walked around the village together, visiting the *peñas* with their homemade wine and laughing and talking together. Oh, about life and what she wanted to do when she finished at school and such things. And as dawn approached I walked her back to her house which was on the edge of the village. It was in some woods and as we neared the gate at the end of the driveway she pulled me into the trees and undressed me. Just like that. It was a dark night. There was no moon. Just the stars to watch our lovemaking. The next day we met early and she drove us into the Castilian plains. We visited Pedraza which is a beautiful walled village. Then it was back to her village for lunch with my friends. I remember we had roast suckling pig which the owner of the restaurant divided into quarters with the blunt edges of two plates, to show how tender the flesh was. I didn't go to the *corrida* that day, but sat on the edge of the square, drinking iced espresso, watching the bulls' carcasses being carried out in the bucket of an earthmover. At nine we met again. We were coming out of some bar and suddenly the glass in my hand was slapped away and an angry man was screaming at me in Spanish. Justina, she jumped between us and tried to calm him. It was her brother, you see, and he was very unhappy that his sister should be with a foreigner. Anyway, he dragged her away and I never saw her again.'

Angelo sighed and stared into space thoughtfully. No one spoke for a few moments and then Thompson said, 'Bloody hell, you're a bundle of laughs. Mind you, I could have told you that. I've lost count of the number of fights I've been in with Spanish blokes just because their sisters were looking for a good shafting. Hanna, are you all right? You haven't touched that beer. It's OK, isn't it? I thought you said you liked beer.'

'Yes,' she said, 'but I think I would like to drink a coffee because I am quite tired.'

'Barman, can you fix a coffee for her?'

'Of course. It's no problem. I just have to go to the kitchens because this machine is not working tonight. Don't ask me why, but there is always something in this place which doesn't work and tonight it's the turn of the coffee machine here. It can't be helped and it's no problem, in any case.'

'I'll come with you, Uncle Angelo,' said Hanna.

'Uncle? He's your uncle?'

She laughed. 'Not really, but everyone calls him Uncle Angelo. It is like your name, now.'

Then she kissed Thompson on the cheek and followed Angelo across the lobby and through the restaurant to the kitchens. She smiled at me on the way but did not say anything. When they had gone I put two logs on the fire and listened to Thompson and Nichol.

'What was that bloody bloke on about, anyway?' asked Thompson.

'Search me. He's hardly stopped since I got back here.'

'He sounds like a bloody socialist to me, all that crap about profits. It's all right for him. He hasn't got overheads to worry about. He wouldn't know a bloody overhead if it landed on his head.'

'He's not hurting anyone. Some people can live without overheads.'

'And some people can live with them. It just takes a bit of common sense. A bit of nous, that's all. And none of that commie shit. And what does he look like as well. Hotel, it's a bloody circus. Tell you what, though, Hanna's bloody marvellous, isn't she. First time out, if you can believe it. I was giving Uschi, her sister, I was giving her a quick whirl earlier, and in walks Hanna, all ready for bed. Oh, sorry, she says. Well, I wasn't going to let that go, was I. So I had a word with her mum. Haven't cracked it yet. I thought I might take a shower first. You gotta have some respect, after all. First time and all that.'

'First time for everything,' said Nichol.

'I can't decide whether to eat first or to take her upstairs right now. What do you think?'

I stopped listening and stared at the flames which were quite big and hot. Some bits of burning wood landed on the carpet and I had to pick them up quickly with my hands but it was too late to take a log off so I just left it and hoped it would not get too hot.

Aside from Rafael, the sculptor, and my captain, Elisa had only one regular client. His name was Antonio. He was a thin, unhealthy man who worked as an agent for the Communist Party in the countryside around Como. I knew him but he did not know about my relationship with Elisa and I never told her that once every couple of weeks Antonio and I would go for a beer together in a place on the Via C—. 'There's this whore I visit,' he would say. 'Elisa. I've mentioned her perhaps. Oh, but she's something. She rips me up with her body and her eyes, tits which sit up and beg and a laugh that sounds like a fountain in springtime. Every time I see her I tell her, why are you doing this, what is it with you. Leave all this and marry me. I'll take you away from it all. But she tears me apart. Why should I give this up, she says. What can you give me that I don't have already? Money? I earn more in a week than you do in a year. Sex? Ha, that's a good one. What can you offer me, Antonio? Love, I say to her. I can give you all the love in the world. And you're telling me you enjoy this job? I've seen some of the men who come here. Oh, but Andreas, she's smart. She rips me up. And what would I do, she always says, with a husband who goes to the brothel three times a week? What would I do with a lover who falls in love with whores? What sort of a man are you if you're so sad you have to pay money to be with a woman? And you think it's a compliment to be loved by such a man? Ha, it's an insult. Time's up, she always says. Get lost. Then she throws me out of her room as if I'm nothing to her. Nothing at all, though I take her flowers, I take her *bijoux*, I am tender with her. I don't know what to do.'

I would never say much. It seemed to be enough for him to have a man he could speak to about it and I was interested to hear what he had to say. It was a privilege because normally other men don't tell you what they think of your lovers. One time when I met him his face was flushed and he was upset. 'It's Elisa,' he said. 'She has a lover. Don't ask me how I know, but I'm sure of it. I said to her, do you always make the men you sleep with use a condom and she said, yes, of course, it's only sensible. So then I said that surely it would not matter if she were to be with one man without using a condom. No, she said. One man would not matter. Not if she was sure of him. I was very excited as you can guess, but then she told me that I was not the man. I left. I paid her and I left. I cannot face it any more, to know that there is a man in the world who possesses her in a way that I cannot.' I tried to calm him but the more he talked the more upset he became. Finally, he stood and said to me, 'Enough. I am a man. I will go to the brothel now and I will pick her up and carry her away with me. You'll see. Wait here and I shall bring her here to show you.' After he had gone I was not sure what to do but I decided to drink another beer and wait to see if he would come back. An hour passed and then another but there was no sign of Antonio so finally I left. When I got home Elisa was there. She was more quiet than usual, but she did not mention any trouble at Number

70

Sixty-Nine and I could not ask.

A fortnight passed, then a month, then six and still I had heard nothing of Antonio. I had nearly forgotten him, but then, one day as the winter was setting in, I went to the bar where we used to meet. I had not been there for a while and I do not know why I went, but he was there, dressed in a sharp suit, suntanned, and wearing sunglasses although the sky was overcast and there was a thin rain. When he saw me he waved me over. '*Ciao* Andreas,' he said. 'I'm just passing through. I have business in Lugano.' The way he said the word 'business' made me want to laugh. 'Sit,' he said. 'Join me for a glass of champagne. Tell me your news.' There was not much to tell him and I was, in any case, not used to telling him anything, but we spoke together for a short time until another man came in and whispered in his ear and he got up to leave. 'I am not a man to bear grudges,' he said. 'And you were a friend to me when I was weak. Give her my regards.' With that he left and I never heard of him again. Elisa, though, heard from him once, soon after I had seen him. She received a package through the post and inside was a piece of rock and a postcard of Vesuvius with an inscription on the back: 'Who can hold fire in his hand by thinking on the frosty Caucasus?'

As my uncle came back through, he hesitated as he passed me and looked around. Thompson asked him, 'You all right, barman?'

'It's this hotel,' my uncle said. 'As I told you, it is on the site of the old sanatorium. People say that the dead still walk here at night. It is nonsense, of course. To believe in ghosts is nonsense. In the night, though . . .'

Hanna said, 'But it's true, there are ghosts. Uschi has seen them. On clear nights when the moon is full they come out and dance through the village. She has seen them, she swears it.'

Thompson smiled at her and put his arm around her shoulders. Then he took a metal tube out of his pocket and took a cigar out of the tube. 'Barman,' he said. 'You got any matches there?'

Angelo ignored him because he was busy looking at the music on the jukebox. Hanna reached over the bar and picked up Manuel's lighter.

'Thank you, my dear. At least someone around here knows the meaning of the word "service".'

He nudged Nichol who shook his head. Angelo turned round and looked at them both.

'Aha, so you found a light,' he said. 'It is a Cuban cigar, am I right? Once I smoked cigars, but they seem pretentious to me now. That's not to say that you are pretentious, of course, but you need to have a certain air about you to get away with it. For myself cigarettes are better, or chewing tobacco when I'm on my own. Manuel, he's proud to be a worker. A Spanish worker. So he smokes workers' cigarettes. Me, I am also a worker, but perhaps a worker-intellectual of some sort, if I can say that. So I smoke worker-intellectual cigarettes which is to say that they are a worker's cigarettes but they are a little more expensive. It's a strange way to define your position in life, I suppose, but still. Look, it has already gone time to put the clock forward. Excuse me and do not forget your wristwatches.'

He walked over to the entrance and started to climb on to the stool he had taken with him, but Thompson said, 'No, leave it. Put it forward when I've gone to bed. Not yet.'

'But the time . . .'

Thompson stood and moved towards Angelo and Nichol stood as well.

'Just leave it, I said. Don't you listen to people? It's psychological, isn't it. If the clock says two we'll all feel like it's an hour later. I'd rather you put it back an hour and then we'd feel like it was an hour earlier. Leave it.'

Angelo looked over at me and raised his eyebrows but he put the stool back at the bar without changing the time.

'As you wish,' he said. 'For me it is unimportant. When I wake up the guests who have asked for alarm calls they will only complain anyway because they will think it is too early. It's a pain in the arse if you ask my opinion. If I don't wake them they'll still complain, but not to me. What do I care? I'll

74

still finish my work an hour earlier than usual, whatever time the clock shows. If everyone agrees what the time is, after all, there's not much point in pretending they're all wrong and you are right. Breakfast will still be served at their time and not at your time. One clock in the world won't make much difference to it.'

One night I was woken by the doorbell. At first I thought that Elisa had answered it because she was not beside me in bed. But the bell kept ringing and finally I answered it to find Elisa, wrapped in a blanket, with a policeman on either side of her. 'You should look after your wife, friend. It's not good for a woman to walk the streets naked at night, whatever her profession.' They laughed. A week later something must have disturbed me when she left, because when I ran down the stairs I caught her at the door. I led her back to bed. What are you looking for, Elisa? I asked her. 'I am looking for the moon,' she said. 'I want to sail on the Sea of Tranquillity.' In the morning when she awoke she remembered nothing of it.

'What was that? I heard something. Over there.' Nichol stood and looked around the lobby.

'Just the fire,' said Angelo. 'Just a log on the fire. The heat, it splits them.'

Nichol shook his head and walked a few steps away from the bar.

'Or one of our ghosts.'

Angelo winked at Hanna and she smiled.

'Quiet!' said Nichol.

Far away a door slammed and there was the sound of laughter. Then the gears of the lift started up. The lift doors opened and Manuel and Alexandra fell out on to the lobby floor, giggling and shushing each other. Nichol relaxed and sat down again and Thompson stood up and said, 'Manuel, my old mate. About bloody time. I've been waiting for one of your cocktails for about six bloody hours now, so get your arse over the other side of that bar and get mixing. All right Alex? He been keeping you hard at it, has he?'

Alexandra giggled again and pulled Manuel across the room. He held Nichol's shoulder when he reached him and tried to stand up straight. Then he walked round to take Angelo's place behind the bar and said, 'So, you wanna cocktail. Where's Bernie? Where's my book?'

Manuel picked up the cocktail book from the bar-top where Alexandra had left it but Thompson grabbed it from his hands and started looking through it.

'What's this, then?' he said. 'An A to Z of cocktails. This any good? Tell you what, let's start at A and work our way through to Z.'

'It's not an A to Z,' said Manuel. 'Some letters aren't included.'

Thompson waved the comment away and quickly read a couple of pages.

'I'll have this Adam's Apple one. Hanna, you're on B, Alexandra C, Jim D, Manuel E . . .'

'There's no E.'

'Shut the fuck up and mix a drink, will you? Night porter, are you in on this?' Angelo did not answer or even look at Thompson. 'And you can put the lot on my tab. Everything we drink tonight. My treat. Do we have to listen to this crap, by the way? What about something we can dance to. I fancy a dance. Are you pouring me a drink, Manuel, or what?'

'You have to read me the recipe.'

'Read it your bloody self. I've got better things on my mind and what do you think you're paid for anyway?' He turned on his stool to face Hanna and kissed her.

Angelo tapped Manuel's shoulder and pointed at a bottle of gin on the shelf and Manuel passed it to him. Angelo filled his glass again and then walked over to the reception desk where he sat down. Then I decided to have another beer and went and got one. Thompson stared at me and I stared back at him but we did not say anything. I opened the beer with my teeth. Nichol laughed and took the drink Manuel had

78

made him and tapped Thompson on the shoulder.

'I'm going to crash for a while,' he said. 'Over by the fire. Is that OK?'

'Yeah, all right Jim. You're a good man. Long day tomorrow. I'd let you go, but you never know what'll come up.'

Nichol sat down in the armchair opposite the one I had been sitting in before and closed his eyes straight away. I did not feel like sitting with him, so I went round the bar and sat on a stool next to Hanna. She touched my knee when Thompson was not looking and I smiled at her. Manuel was making his own drink and when it was ready he came round too and sat next to Alexandra so the five of us were in a line.

'Hey,' said Manuel.

Thompson ignored him for a moment, then turned to face him.

Manuel said, 'What do you think? Do you like it?'

'Not bad at all, mate. It's got a certain *je ne sais quoi*. What's in it again?'

'Calvados, Martini, Gordon's, yellow Chartreuse, lemon peel and a cherry.'

'Yeah, I gave the cherry to Hanna. I can't stand cherries. Well, not this sort.'

'These are good cherries, from USA. Fresh, ripe. They're flown in especially.'

'Can't be helped. If you don't like something, there's no good eating it, is there? Tell you what, though. I could do with a bite to eat. All this exercise has made me hungry.'

'What do you like? You name it, we fix it.'

'Yeah? Reckon you can manage some fresh anchovies? Or a swordfish steak?'

'It's possible, yes. We'll see. Soon we can look in the kitchens and see what there is.'

Thompson pulled Hanna's hand from his leg and said, 'Take a walk for a minute, there's a good girl.'

She slipped off her stool and went over to the reception desk and sat on the corner of it, swinging her leg and staring out of the window. Alexandra joined her a moment later and sat on the desk in front of my uncle then both of them got down again and went to the ladies' cloakroom.

Thompson stared at me but I did not see why I should move and stayed where I was. Thompson turned his back to me. Then he moved on to the stool next to Manuel and took another cigar from his pocket and handed it to Manuel who sniffed it and clipped the end and then lit it with his lighter.

'Tell you what, Manuel,' said Thompson. 'I could use a decent barman in Malaga, if you're interested.'

'In Malaga. Cocktails?' Manuel asked.

'Yeah, cocktails. This sort of shit. Classics, not all that poncey rubbish with umbrellas in it. Real cocktails. What it is, I've just got hold of this big building in the hills outside town, just bought it. It's a prime bit of real estate, as a matter of fact. It used to be a restaurant, so the layout's all there already, and I want to turn it into an American bar. You know, Casablanca and all that stuff. Live piano, casino, cocktails, the works. Make it classy, you know. The sort of place people are going to make the effort to visit if they live down on the coast. Well, it's up to you. I can't see the attraction of this place, I have to say. It's a bit quiet for my taste, and I would have though it was for a man of your calibre as well. What do you think?'

'When do I start?'

Thompson did not answer for a moment and then said, 'That's a bit difficult to say. I've got a few things to sort out before I start developing it. A few things to clear up. But if you're keen I'll let you know.'

'Sure. Like you say, this place is quiet. Yes, a good job near home, I'd like that.'

'So why do you work here, anyway? I mean, if I was you, I'd find something in Spain. There must be some decent hotels which need people like you.'

'Sure, but they aren't as good with the money, you know. Here we get good guests. Lots of money, good tips. Americans, they tip good. Film stars, princes, everyone. They all come to Hotel Weissman.'

'Yeah? So where are they all?'

Manuel laughed. 'Sleeping. No, really, it's late in the season for us. The snow here, it does strange things at this time of year and the skiing is very dangerous. There are many avalanches.'

As he said this there was a roll of thunder in the distance and Manuel laughed again. 'You see? You can imagine, only the professionals come at this time of year. But in February you should see it. There are hundreds of people. We have to hire two extra helicopters. They are more like buses, there are so many people to take up to the mountain tops. I can tell you, it's a big party. In one week I can make what I would earn in a year in Spain. Even Angelo gets good tips and he never sees any guests.'

'It sounds like a good racket. Are you sure you want a job?'

Manuel looked around to check that Alexandra had not come back in.

'My wife, you know. And the little ones. I miss them. And also it is not good for a Spanish man to leave his woman behind like this. They talk about me, really, the people from our neighbourhood. Although it is very important for the Spanish man to be free and strong, he has his responsibilities, you understand? And to tell the truth I hate this place.

Even though I earn a lot of money in the high season, I just spend it anyway. I like my women, you understand, and my cigarettes and my drink. These things are important, of course they are. But to tell you the truth, they are fucking expensive in this part of the world. I can earn more, but to earn more I have to spend more. It is, how do you call it, Catch 22.'

'Yeah, it's not good,' said Thompson. 'I know the problem. Look at me. To get anywhere with my business you've got to drive a Porsche at least. And even then, I've met people who won't deal with you unless you roll up in a Ferrari or a Lamborghini. Overheads. It's all bloody overheads. Like paying people like him and Davy to traipse across Europe with me. There's always a payoff. It can't be helped, though.'

'It is the necessities of life. What can you do?'

Thompson stood up and faced Manuel and held his shoulder with his left hand and held out his right hand for Manuel to shake.

'You're all right, Manuel. You're a sound man. But I tell you what – my glass is empty.'

Alexandra and Hanna came back and Thompson waved them across while Manuel went back behind the bar and picked up his book.

'OK,' he said. 'I can give you a Gibson Cocktail – that's a dry Martini with garlic instead of orange peel' – Thompson screwed up his face – 'or a Gin Cocktail, but that has a cherry and so does a Great Guns Cocktail and, in fact, so does a Gangster Cocktail. And that's all the ones with a G. Better take your pick: a cherry or garlic.'

'What else is in a Gangster Cocktail?'

'Let's see. Brandy, brown curaçao, lemon peel. Pretty good. And Bernie says: This is quite a strong cocktail and should not be drunk on an empty stomach. Of course, sometimes he exaggerates, but usually it's the truth enough.'

'I'll take your word for it. And I certainly don't want bloody garlic in my drink. I hate garlic. Give me one of those Gangster jobs. Just skip the cherry. So Hanna, what's going on?'

'It's snowing,' she said. 'It's good. I like it. It's so fresh. I like it. It makes me want to go out and play in it.'

'Aren't you drinking that? let me taste it. It's warm. Do you want another?'

'No, I can't drink these. They make me sleepy. I'd like a glass of water, though. I'm thirsty.'

'Get her a glass of water, Manuel. And do excuse me. I've got to piss. Oh, by the way, can I make a phone call from down here or do I have to go to my room?'

'Sure. Andreas or Angelo, they can fix a line for you. You can use one of the cabins.'

Thompson went across to the reception desk and took a sheet of notepaper which he wrote something on. And then he said to my uncle, 'Do us a favour, mate. Get me Mr Mace on that number here. That's Mace. Tell him to hold on, OK?'

Then he went to the toilets while Angelo dialled the number. Angelo asked for Mr Mace and then said, 'Mr Mace, I have a call for you, long distance from Italy, from the Hotel Weissman, a Mr Thompson.' Then Angelo asked him to hold on and put the call through to cabin two which was furthest from the fireplace, but Nichol still woke up when he heard the ringing. Angelo winked at me. When Thompson came back he went into the cabin and picked up the phone.

When he finished he slammed the receiver down and banged the door behind him. Nichol asked him, 'What is it, Boss?'

Thompson ignored him and walked straight over to the bar

and Nichol joined him.

'It really pisses me off,' Thompson said. 'You bloody leave a bloke in charge and he cocks it up. I'm going to bloody fire that bloke when we get to Malaga. I've had enough of him.'

'So what's up?'

'I told him not to pay out on the Marrakesh deal until three months were up, and I told him they'd probably get heavy on him. So yesterday they sent some of their boys round looking for me, had a word with Mace, and he only gave them a bloody cheque. I just don't believe it. Boss, he says, they were gents. They're short on cash and I negotiated a reduction in return. Well, I said to him, you don't negotiate reductions after the event. You negotiate a reduction the next time when you promise to pay the bastards quicker. He hasn't got a bloody clue.'

Angelo crossed to the bar and sat next to Thompson. 'You see, this is why I have no interest in the business world for myself. There are far too many complications . . .'

Thompson whipped round and grabbed Angelo by the lapels, choking him, and lifted him off the stool. 'You just shut your mouth and do your job you poncey socialist bastard. I've had enough of you, got it?'

Angelo nodded and Thompson relaxed his grip slightly, then tightened it again. 'And another thing. Stop listening to my private conversations. Got it?'

My uncle nodded again and Thompson let him go. He stumbled over to the reception desk and slumped over it. No one said anything. Then Hanna and Alexandra went running over to Angelo and put their arms around him while he tried to catch his breath. I stayed where I was and just stared at Thompson who looked at me and then turned away.

'Why did you do that?' asked Hanna. Thompson did not answer and turned away from her. 'Do you want some air?'

she asked my uncle. Angelo nodded and the three of them went to the entrance and stood in the porchway.

'Manuel, make sure he's OK, will you. I want a word with Jim. And you can take a fucking walk as well. You're pissing me off sitting there.'

Manuel put a hand on my shoulder and led me outside before I could say anything back. I stood and watched Hanna and Alexandra while they looked after my uncle, and Manuel and I shared his cigar because I had left my cigarettes on the bar. It was cold in the porch and I wanted to go back in but Manuel told me to stay for a while longer, until Angelo was ready to go in too. After we had been out there for five minutes, though, I told Manuel to get out of my way and went inside and straight through to the kitchens. On the way I heard Thompson say, 'Put that bloody clock forward, will you. The sooner tonight ends the better.'

I did not want anything in the kitchens but it was warmer there and I would not have to watch my uncle. Then I decided to get a knife from one of the knife-racks. I chose a small paring knife and wrapped it in cloth before I slipped it inside my boot. If Thompson attacked me, I thought, I would be ready for him. Elisa always complained about the fact that I carried a knife with me wherever we went in Como. 'It's stupid. If they see you have a knife, they will come back another time with a gun. If they have a knife and you have one they are more likely to use it. It's very obvious to me.' But at other times I would be in the kitchen preparing a meal and she would come in, naked, and hand me a knife, whichever one she liked the look of, and put it in my hand. She would guide my hand, running the sharp edge of the blade over her skin, around her neck, across her breasts, down her stomach and her thighs. 'Do it. A little harder. A little harder. More. Break the skin. Ah, yes. More.'

When I went back through, Angelo and Nichol were sitting in the armchairs by the fire. Nichol seemed restless and uncomfortable and I went over and sat in the chair next to his. Hanna was sitting next to Thompson but she did not speak to him or look at him. He asked her, 'Hey, do you want a drink?' She did not answer. 'All right,' he said. 'I'm sorry. I lost my temper.'

'Tell Uncle Angelo, not me,' she said.

'Yeah, yeah, I'll tell him. I'll make it up to him.'

'You shouldn't have done that. He was only being friendly. He is a good man.'

'All right, keep your hair on. I said, I'll make it up to him in a while. Let me finish my drink, that's all.'

Thompson's face was red and wet with sweat. He loosened his tie and undid the top button of his shirt. Manuel and Alexandra came back inside a minute later. They were covered in snow and laughing.

'You two are like a bunch of kids,' said Thompson. 'Is it still snowing out there?'

'Snowing, yes, much snow. You'll be here longer than you think,' said Alexandra.

'You are joking, I hope.'

'Sure, it's one metre already tonight and in the passes there will be deep drifts because of the wind. Also there may be more avalanches. Then it should take even longer to clear some of the roads. And if the wind is going the wrong way, some of the tunnels may fill. It's difficult to say. It has been worse, but still no one will be going anywhere tomorrow, I think.'

'What about the helicopter?'

'Perhaps, if the snow has stopped and the wind isn't so strong, but listen to it. Perhaps, maybe, who can tell. But don't worry, Manuel can tell you. When there is snow like this the hotel has lots of food, drink, even your cigars. It's no problem. We'll have a party. Always if the guests are stuck here there is a big party. The insurance people, I think, they pay for it all.'

88

'I can't hang around here. I've got to be in Venice by lunchtime tomorrow. Or today, I should say.'

'Well, you could be lucky with the helicopter. But I don't think the wind will stop. Two, three days it will snow, I think. I have seen this before. It is freak weather, but not such a freak. Anyway, you are lucky that Hanna and I will have to stay here too. It is not even possible to get down to the village when it is like this. Unless you can ski, anyway. Hanna, your make-up. Come with me, I'll fix it.'

Thompson called to Nichol, 'Did you hear that? What are we going to do?'

Nichol shrugged. 'Perhaps it'll be OK. Give them a call. Or Mace, call him. Postpone the meeting for a couple of days.'

'I can't do that. Christ, this is just what I need. This is too good.' He stood up and started walking around the lobby. 'Manuel,' he said. 'When will we know if the helicopter can fly?'

'In the morning, of course. Well, it suits me. I can have a decent sleep here and a proper shower in the morning, instead of that fucking bath in the staff chalet. Angelo, did you tell your brother what I said? That if you don't get out of the bath before you pull the plug you end up with shit and piss all over you. It's a disgrace. Hey, mate, what's the problem? Take it easy. Have a drink. It's all right. There's nothing you can do about it, you know. In the morning we'll see and if you have to you can call your friends or whatever.'

'Don't tell me to take it easy you spic ponce. You're talking about my business.'

Thompson went back to the bar and took one of Manuel's cigarettes and lit it. He coughed and stubbed it out again.

'What the hell are these,' he said. 'Jim, give us a cigarette.'

Then he walked over to the fireplace again and sat on the sofa opposite me. He looked at me and I stared back.

'What's your name?' he asked me.

'Andreas.'

'Scrawny little bastard, aren't you. You shouldn't be out so late, that's why.'

He stood up and walked around the lobby, punching his right hand into the palm of his left. Then he took off his jacket and threw it to Nichol who put it on the back of a chair. Thompson's shirt was dark with sweat on his back and under his arms. Slowly he rolled up his shirt-sleeves. Then he went to the bar and picked up Manuel's cocktail book and looked through some pages.

'This bloke's a bloody comedian,' he said.

'He's the best. Bernie's the king,' said Manuel.

'Bloody queen, more like it.'

'Bernie has style. He's a craftsman, an artisan.'

'Yeah, that's just what the world needs, a bunch of bloody artisans. I can do without artisans, myself. You're as bad as he is. You're *plein de merde*, you are. *Plein de* fucking *merde*. Well. I'll tell you what I want now: a straight single malt scotch with no cherries, no umbrellas, no ice and no poncey bullshit.'

'Coming up,' said Manuel.

'I have to say, though,' Thompson went on, 'I have got simple tastes as a rule. I like good stuff, but I like it simple. A good cigar, a good drink, a good bit of food. I mean, even a good drink's complicated enough, if you think about it. And look what happens when you try and complicate things. You get cock-ups. If we'd gone straight to Venice instead of coming here I wouldn't be in this mess, for a start. Or take my old chef. Ramon, he was a fat git. There was nothing he liked more than making things complicated. He was always trying out something complicated in the kitchen, and every single time he cocked it up. I sacked him. Couldn't be bothered

with it, could I, so I've got this old dear coming in now.
English. Knows her stuff and she doesn't try to make things
hard for herself, know what I mean? And my business manager, Mace, he's got something wrong in his head, if you ask
me. I remember when he started as my assistant. I couldn't
believe it, the way he wanted to piss about with front com-
panies and offshore this and that and bits of bloody paper
everywhere. Keep things simple, I said to him. Then you
know where you stand. No point in being a millionaire if you
don't know where all your money is, is there? Diversify, he's
always saying. Complicate, I say. It's all about core business.
Keep those overheads down, Mace, I keep telling him. Stick
to what you're good at. It's like you, Manuel, you complicate
all these drinks, but I don't suppose even you would put
twenty-year-old port in a cocktail, would you? No, don't
answer that. I don't want to know. I'll tell you what, though,
there's times when things need to be a bit more complicated,
if you ask me. Look at this hotel. I mean, you're sitting on a
goldmine here and you're not digging. What have you got.
Half a dozen cafés, this bar, a helicopter and some hotels.
What about the kids? There's nothing here for the kids. And
what about a jacuzzi or some indoor tennis courts or something? It's all right, keeping things simple, but you can go too
far, after all. This place needs a bit of investment, some
facilities. It's no good having a place like this without any
facilities, is it. Whoever runs this place keeps things too simple. That would be like running a bar which only sold beer,
wouldn't it. Simple, all right, but bloody boring. Maybe I'll
have a word with your manager before I go tomorrow. See
what he's got to say for himself.'

Hanna and Alexandra had come back while Thompson
was talking. He stared at them.

'I think I'd better go and have a shower. I'm a bit tired and it'll wake me up. The night's still young. You wait here, OK? And when I get back I want to see the manager about this weather. I can't hang about here. I've got business to attend to.'

He got off his stool, walked to the fireplace and picked up his jacket and then shouted to Nichol, 'Jim. Upstairs.'

Nichol followed him into the lift and they went.

After they had gone, Angelo got up and went over to the bar and held out his empty glass in front of him. Manuel took the glass and filled it and Hanna pulled Angelo on to the stool were Thompson had been sitting.

'This has been an eventful night,' Angelo said and the others laughed. 'And normally things are so peaceful here, just me and the ghosts. Your health. Though, in my opinion, the three of you look a little like ghosts in any case, with your white faces and your tired eyes. Did you know, Hanna, that ghosts have tired eyes? It's obvious, if you stay up all night and then try to sleep when the rest of the world is awake your eyes get tired. It can't be helped. Even my eyes, as you can see, get tired. I have seen so many nights.'

Manuel opened beers for himself and Hanna and Alexandra, and Hanna came over to me and handed me her bottle.

'I don't want it,' she said. 'Would you like it?'

I took it and thanked her and she sat down in the armchair next to mine. Then the others joined us there and Manuel put some more logs on to the fire.

'I have seen so many nights,' said Angelo again. 'Sometimes you come to wonder if you have become a ghost yourself. If death has maybe surprised you and taken you away without your realizing it. It could happen. How would we know, after all. Who are we to say that each of us has not already died a dozen deaths, a thousand deaths, for all we know. You can imagine it. In one life you are killed. You leave others behind and they mourn your death. But in the instant of your death in that life a new dimension is created where you are still alive, where all those who knew you before are there, but perhaps slightly, very slightly different. Not even different enough for you to notice, but different enough to be not exactly the same people you left behind when you died. How would we know? The Christians, they say it is a matter of faith that there is a heaven. But sometimes I think it is a matter of faith that the earth we inhabit today is the same as the one we inhabited yesterday. How can you tell, I ask you. Saledin, he was always ready to talk about these things. But he's dead now. It depends on how you see things, I suppose. Cause and effect, I would say to him. The will of God, he would reply. I hit you and you fall down, I'd say. God in his infinite, inscrutable wisdom wills your fist into contact with my jaw and wills my body into contact with the earth, he'd say. There's no arguing with such a man.' He gulped down his gin.

'Don't cry,' said Hanna. I had not noticed the tears on my uncle's cheek. 'I hate it when you cry,' she said.

There was a choked sob as Angelo buried his head in his hands and Hanna hugged him. I glanced at Manuel and Alexandra. They were holding hands, and I was surprised to see Alexandra take out her handkerchief, dab her eyes with it and give it to Manuel who did the same after shaking it out and folding it neatly.

Angelo looked around on the floor and pointed at Alexandra's bottle of beer.

'Give it to me,' he said. He sucked on it and gulped, shook his head so that his hair fell over his eyes, breathed deeply for a few seconds and nodded. 'It is well. Listen. It would be a bad night to spend on the mountains. They are taking off their winter coats. It's best not to be in the way.'

Again, nearer this time, perhaps in the valley, there was the crashing of snow on the mountainsides.

'Stoke the fire, Manuel. Build it bright and hot. To die of cold would be a terrible thing.' He sucked again on his beer. 'Hanna, give me one of Manuel's cigarettes. On the bar.'

She fetched them straightaway and said, 'Here, let me light it for you. Are you OK now? I wonder if they'll come back. He's drunk now, isn't he? He might fall asleep.' She hesitated and Alexandra frowned at her. 'He won't come back, will he?' Hanna said. 'And we're stuck here tonight.'

'There are worse places, Hanna. Look at your face. Oh, dear, and mine as well, I suppose. Come on. Again.'

Alexandra pulled Hanna to her feet and they went to the ladies' room but came back soon afterwards. They sat at the bar and talked quietly. For a long time Angelo and Manuel and I stayed quiet and still, only stirring when there was the sound of another avalanche in the distance.

M anuel got another beer for himself and Angelo but I did not want one.

'Thank you,' said Angelo. 'I see that Mr Thompson has put the clock forward, after all. The weight of time, or maybe just knowledge, it must have subdued him in one way, at least. I recall in Vienna I had an acquaintance. A good man. His name was Rudi and he ran a small bar. Have I mentioned him? We were great drinking partners, Rudi and I. We got on well enough. He was from Salzburgerland, a farm worker. He won the money for the bar from an aristocrat in a fencing contest. The aristocrat – you would know the story if you'd been here at the time because the newspapers were full of it – he couldn't believe that someone from the land, a peasant, could beat him in a fencing contest. He was an arrogant young man, as Rudi told it to me, who had studied at Heidelberg and been top fencer in his fraternity or some such nonsense. He and Rudi had an argument, this was in Vienna, and Rudi said to him, I see from your face that you can fence. Let's settle it that way. Of course, the aristocrat accepted; he had to under the circumstances. And he

97

suggested in addition that they put money on the outcome: Rudi's beaten-up old car for the aristocrat's Mercedes. Ha, the aristocrat was skating on thin ice. He was playing with fire. They fought and Rudi won. If the aristocrat had not been so obsessed with his code he would have realized. For Rudi it was not a matter of honour or style to have scars on his face, but not to have them. What the aristocrat took for inexperience was, in fact, excellence. So, Rudi bought a bar with the money he got from selling the Mercedes and found a taste for betting at the same time. He would bet on anything with anyone. And the bet was always for the same thing: the loser would have to buy two bottles of wine and they would fill two huge brandy glasses and drink one bottle each, down in one. I had to be carried out of that place more times than I care to remember, which is obvious if you think about it. Rudi, well, eventually the weight of time subdued him, as well. He had discovered his own code of honour for his life: to drink as much as he was challenged to. And he died soon after I last saw him. Manuel, there is a moral in this story: honour is important, but it shouldn't be confused with obligation. And that's all I have to say on the matter.'

'What sort of wine did he drink?' asked Manuel.

'Only the worst if he won or the best if he lost. Of course, there was more to it than that. There always is to drinking. If you know you're in a cage you'll want to get out. It's the way people are. And if you can't get out the next best thing is to drink yourself into oblivion so you don't know the cage is there in the first place. I've done it often enough myself.'

Manuel smiled and they were quiet again. Then Angelo moved from his seat and sat next to me and said, 'So, Andreas. Another night. Perhaps you can sense the routine. It is the routine which makes things work here. You have to get used to it. Every night is different, but every night is the same. Our universe is fragile and when you sit here every night from dusk until dawn you come to realize that. The night, its latticing unfolds for you. It shows itself for what it is. Something crystalline. Precise and cold and brittle. When you're here on your own, of course, you appreciate it more. You come to feel as if it is a crystal, as if you are the seed at its heart. You'll learn that. You'll have plenty of time to learn. Plenty of nights. It gives you time to think. That's the least you can say for it. Time to think and imagine things, if that's your taste.'

Manuel broke in, 'But he can't stay here for ever, Angelo. It's OK for you to say, you've travelled. You've seen the world. Andreas hasn't. The boy has to see some of the world. You can't count the military, after all. Then he can come back here. Don't you think, Andreas? You are always welcome in Seville, you should know that. And one or two other places I can think of where I have friends who'll always look out for me if I ask them to do something. You remember that. You can't spend your life sitting on your ass up here in the mountains.'

'You say that, Manuel Moreno, but what has travelling around the world ever done for me? Look at me, I go away for a few years and everything's different when I come back. When I leave there's a hospital here, a wonderful place where people can rest. And now look at it. A playboy hotel with rich bitches and bastards all over it like flies. No, if you ask me, it's not worth it.'

'But can you imagine sitting here every night with nothing to think about? You'd go out of your mind. And you wouldn't be here now if you didn't have your stupid stories to tell, would you?'

'You could be right. You have to live in the world to

think anything of it. But it reminds me of a man I met once, an American of Sicilian extraction . . .'

Alexandra stamped her feet and shrieked, 'But enough now, Angelo. Please. Save this story for another night.'

Angelo opened his mouth as if to say something, then closed it again, looked at Manuel and then me and shrugged. Manuel laughed and shook his head but he did not say anything and neither did I. Then Alexandra came over and pulled Manuel up from his seat and tried to lead him in a dance but he would not and shrugged her off. Then she whispered in his ear and he said, 'Again? You gonna kill me, but OK.' And they left.

Angelo stretched in his seat, then got up and stretched again and said he was going to take a walk around the complex but that I should stay with Hanna in case Thompson came back and wanted another drink. I said OK and when my uncle had gone I went and got another bottle of beer and sat next to Hanna at the bar.

'How's it going?' she asked me.

I shrugged and told her that it was going quite well but that it was boring. And also that I did not like Thompson because of the way he had treated Angelo.

'That was bad,' she said. 'I know. I told him and he said he would apologize. I don't know what was wrong with him. Jim's nice, though. I think he's nice. He's quiet.'

Then I asked if Thompson was being good to her and she said yes, but that she hoped he did not come back. He scared her, she said.

'At least there won't be any school tomorrow,' she said. 'I hope we're snowed in here for a week.'

I told her that I did not think it should be a week, but a few days because the wind was still strong and it was still snowing hard.

'Can I stay in your room?'

'Yes. You haven't seen it. It's one of the old suites turned into two studio apartments so although there is only one room there's enough space. It's quite nice. I like it.'

'Perhaps, if Jonny doesn't come back, maybe I can go there

quite soon, if that's OK with you. I'm tired and I want to take a shower.'

I said that would be fine and that she could sleep in my bed and I would use a sleeping bag and sleep on the sofa. Then I wondered if I should go up and close the french windows which I had forgotten about. I decided I might do it a little later.

'But I won't go yet. I'll wait to see if Jonny comes back. I should, I suppose. Why weren't you in Mario's today?'

'I don't know. I suppose I was not in the mood for it and I was tired from last night. I didn't sleep so well.'

'It must be difficult to sleep, to stay up all night and then to sleep. I don't know how Uncle Angelo does it, though he should be used to it, I suppose. Mario was asking for you. He wants to go to Bolzano with you next week. Can I come?'

'If Alexandra doesn't mind, I don't either. And I suppose Mario will be happy about it. Though you'll have to dress up so you look older. Mario will want to go to a club, I should think.'

Then I said that we should have a coffee if she was going to stay around because it would make her feel better, so we went through to the kitchens.

The kitchens were colder than they should have been and when I went and checked the delivery entrance I found that it was open, so I closed it. Probably my uncle had gone through it and it had not locked after him because the catch was stiff because of the cold. Hanna made the coffee and I leaned against a fridge and smoked a cigarette while I watched her. She looked tired and her hair had lost its shine which made her look ill. The bright red of her lipstick made her skin look white and drawn. I said to her that she should go to bed now because she looked so tired but she just shook her head and put some sugar in my cup without asking me. It tasted nice and not at all bitter, though it was slimy because she had made it so strong. We went back through to the lobby and I decided to add something to my coffee. I asked Hanna if she wanted something in hers as well. She said, yes, so I went behind the bar and poured half a measure of Cointreau and half a measure of cognac into each cup.

'You remembered,' she said.

'Of course. In Como too, we drank it like this if we were cold.'

'We?'

'My friends.'

'Tell me about them.'

'There isn't much to tell. They were OK. Typical Italian, you know.'

'I thought you might write.'

I shrugged and looked away. I had thought about writing to her but it had never seemed important.

'I mean, it doesn't matter. You're back now. But sometimes I wondered.'

We sat next to the fire and I put some more logs on it because it had burnt down a lot since earlier.

'It's good,' said Hanna and I nodded. We did not speak for a while. I held my hands close to the fire because they were cold and then Hanna kneeled down at my feet and did the same.

'Careful,' I said.

She looked up at me and I stroked her hair and she smiled. But when I moved my hand to stroke her neck and cheek she said, 'No, Andreas. Jonny may come back. He has a very bad temper. You have seen it.'

Then Thompson, who must have come down the stairs

very quietly, shouted to her from the other side of the lobby.
'Hanna.'

She stood up right away and pulled her dress straight and
went over to him and he led her through the doors and I listened to their footsteps on the stairs until they were gone.

One of our friends was a local policeman. When he was on
duty Francisco would often come to our apartment for a
meal or just a glass of wine or beer or, if he was in a good
mood, some grappa which he used to bring with him. He
never had sex with Elisa, though he went to Number Sixty-
Nine nearly every day, but he liked to have her serve him
food and drink in her own home while he talked to me. 'For
some men, it is a matter of pride,' he once said to me, 'to
give pleasure to a woman. To make her feel loved and cared
for, wanted for her individual qualities. But I am not such a
man and I detect that you are not either, Weissman. I suspect
that we are the kind of men who think women should be
treated a little differently. For us it is a religious act, an act
of devotion, to treat a woman as far as possible as neither
more nor less than an object. We prefer to worship a woman
as one does the relic at Santa Maria down the road. Or we
like a woman to obey us. To treat us right. We aren't interested in being loved by a woman. If a woman wants to love
us she can, but only as long as she keeps the fact to herself.
If a woman comes out with it, I love you, we're quick to
anger, men like us. We hit her. It doesn't happen often. We
discourage it.' Then he would instruct Elisa to perform some
chore for us. 'Clean our boots now, Elisa. Weissman's first.
Yes, you'll have to take them off. You won't make a proper
job of it otherwise. Give her your foot, Weissman.' Or
another time: 'Go to the shop on the corner for us. Get me
some of my tobacco. Tell the good woman that it is for me.

You won't need money. And Weissman here could do with some more of his cigarettes by the look of it.'

I found it strange, not his behaviour, nor the way he implicated me in it, or the fact that Elisa complied, but that she seemed to enjoy submitting herself to his discipline in this way. Why do you do it? I asked her. I mean, I know you have to do it for your mother's sake, for the street, we all do. But why do you like to do it? 'Oh, but what I like is not to serve him. He is a fat fool, yes, he is. A useful person to have on your side, but most fat fools are useful for something. No, what I like is to see your face when he tells you what sort of man you are. And I like to have the chance to do things for you as well. You are too noble, Andreas. You don't understand that I want to do things for you, even clean your boots as long as you don't expect it of me. I am happy when Francisco comes here to see you. It liberates me from you. When he is here, I am free to be your slave. Otherwise I am not. In any case, I cannot take him seriously. I should not tell you this, but Francisco's thing is to dress as a little baby and be spanked by one of the girls. It is impossible to take such a man seriously.'

I threw the dregs of my coffee into the fire and looked around the lobby. It was quiet. The strip lights seemed dull with no one else around. Again, an avalanche. A big one in the distance. I stood and walked across to the reception desk and looked at the monitors. There was nothing. Just the white corridor walls and the blue carpets. 'Why they decorate a hotel like a hospital I'll never know,' said Angelo when he saw the new colour scheme my father had chosen. 'It's too late for him to be nostalgic about the old place.' But I quite liked it. Our apartment in Como was decorated simply with no carpets, only bare fishbone parquet floors, and on the walls just a few paintings which Elisa's customers had given her. And books everywhere. So many books that often I would have to walk around Elisa's friends, students, who had come to read this novel or that, one history book or another. 'It's better here than in the library,' they would say. 'All the books you want there have already been stolen. You know you'll find them here, at least.'

One of the students, Carlo, was fascinated by Elisa and my relationship with her. Many times, the other students who came to the apartment would invite him to join them at Number Sixty-Nine or one of the other houses in the street, but he would always refuse and stay behind with me for a while. He could not imagine using a prostitute and because he could not imagine it, he could not do it. He was curious, though. 'How does it feel, Andreas, to sleep with a woman who has already had, well, however many men before you that day? I am sure I would feel jealous, or I think I would. I'm not sure. What's it like?' I could not answer his question for him because I did not know what he meant. I asked Elisa what she thought. 'Ah, Carlo, yes, I know about him. It is very simple, really. It is other men he is scared of. Or not scared of them, but scared of intimacy with them, scared of what he might reveal in himself. He worries that he will enjoy the intimacy, that this would reflect on him. He worries that he is gay, and probably he is, but he does not wish to admit this to anyone.' Are you sure, I asked her. 'Yes, I'm sure,' she said.

The hotel was very quiet. Somewhere there was the sound of a door slamming but I could not tell where. I went to the windows and looked out and then went back to the fireplace and sat watching the fire for a while. The wind was stronger and the snow was falling even faster than it had been, so I decided to phone the recorded information service to find out what the weather forecast was, but when I picked up the phone it was dead so I guessed that an avalanche or the wind had knocked down some telegraph poles. I put the phone down and went back to my seat. Just then my uncle came back and I told him about the phone.

'Good,' Angelo said. 'If we're going to be cut off it's better to be cut off properly, otherwise all the guests get nervous and spend their lives phoning people who aren't at all interested in what they have to say. Where have all the people gone?'

I told him that Thompson had come and taken Hanna away and Angelo made a face but smiled when he saw me looking at him.

'Don't worry about Mr Thompson,' he said. 'He is unimportant and I don't want you getting into any trouble with him, whatever you think about it. Come on, let's have another beer. Then we can get some food and relax until it's time to go to bed. Normally I like to have a swim before breakfast because it helps you sleep. Will you swim with me? It would make a change to have some company in the swimming-pool for once.'

I said that I would think about it but that I would probably be tired enough to sleep without going swimming or having any breakfast or anything at all.

'How do you like your rooms?' Angelo asked me. 'It's one of the perks of the job, to get a good room in the hotel instead of having to stay in the staff chalet. It's one of the things my brother didn't change when he changed everything else. You might not remember, but your Uncle Peter and I had a wonderful apartment right at the top of the old house, in the attics. It was as far away from everyone else as possible so we could sleep better in the day. Do you remember the old house?'

'Not very well. I remember when we had to stay in the village while the hotel was being built, but I was quite young.'

'Yes, you were young and you're still young. What do you think about what Manuel says? Would you like to travel for a while, like I did? I can't say I recommend it these days, because when it comes down to it you don't need to travel to see the world. It's all on television and most of it's the same as everywhere else, but I realize it's no good telling a boy like you that. After all, when it comes down to it life wouldn't be worth living if you took any notice of what anyone else said, even if they're right. Manuel's got a point in that respect, at least. What would you like to do? Spain's a good place, if you like that sort of thing. Or you can go to England, if you like. I have friends in England where I worked once. Or Paris, I have friends in Paris. Stockholm, too. I have friends there, even though I never worked there. You can take your pick and I can make it easy for you. Or you can make life difficult for yourself which is what some people prefer. When I was your age I preferred to make life difficult for myself, I know.'

I did not answer for a while because I had not really thought about it. Then there was the sound of Manuel and Alexandra on the stairs and when I turned round they were coming through the doors, laughing as usual.

'You know what we gonna do now,' said Manuel when he reached the bar. 'While that fat asshole's still away, I'm going to make some good drinks for us. What do you say Alexandra? You wanna cocktail?'

I went and sat at the bar next to Alexandra and Angelo came over too. Manuel handed me the book of cocktails. Then he took a bottle of champagne from the wine fridge and opened it. He fired the cork across the room and collected the champagne which spilled out in a glass and drank it. Then he said, 'Daydream, daydream, daydream. Look up Daydream Cocktail and read it.'

I searched through the book and found the recipe he wanted and read it out to him. One teaspoonful of brown Curaçao, one teaspoonful of Angostura bitters, a third of a gill of brandy, one teaspoonful of maraschino, a dash of champagne, a twist of lemon, a cherry and half a tumblerful of broken ice. Half-fill the tumbler with broken ice, add the Curaçao, then put in the Angostura bitters, the brandy and the maraschino. Stir well and pass through a strainer into a cocktail glass. Serve with a dash of champagne, a twist of lemon peel and a cherry.

111

'This is the most expensive cocktail in the book,' said Manuel. 'Because it's obvious: if you need champagne, you have to open a fresh bottle. Because if you want champagne by the glass you can go to Germany. And this is good champagne. Guess who's paying for it. Have anything, he said to me. Put it on my bill, he said. No problem. He's a big spender, Mr Thompson. He's an asshole, but he has money. You want one of these?'

I said, no, I would like a beer because although I do not mind cocktails sometimes I was not in the mood for one now. Angelo said he would have a glass of gin but Alexandra had the cocktail which Manuel had made and then he mixed another for himself.

'Hey, Angelo, how you doing?' said Manuel. 'We're keeping you awake tonight. It makes a change for you, to have some people around you. I shouldn't think it's always like this, though, Andreas. Don't imagine it is. There are whole evenings here when the only people I see are Angelo and whoever is on duty before him. I hate to think what it gets like in the middle of the night. As I say, Jonny Thompson is an asshole, but at least he doesn't go to bed at nine in the evening like all the other assholes who come here, what do you say?'

Angelo grunted and then they went and sat by the fire but I stayed where I was because it was quite nice to be near the windows and watch the snow outside. It was getting deeper which meant that even if it did stop tonight the passes would be blocked and it might take all day for the helicopter pad to be cleared.

After a while I got bored sitting at the bar on my own and I decided to sit with the others by the fire. It was still burning brightly and I sat in the chair nearest to it, turning my face from one side to the other to warm each cheek in turn.

'Andreas, you will dry your skin out,' said Alexandra, but

I did not answer and when I looked round at her a moment later her eyes were closed and she was beginning to snore quietly.

My uncle cleared his throat and said to Manuel, 'My friend, Saledin, in Granada, the philosopher, the Algerian, the one who died recently. He had a saying: We must build a soap factory, he would say. We must build a soap factory to wash away this evil from the world. I dare say he was right, but do you know, to the day he died I will bet he never learnt how to make soap.'

'Angelo, my friend,' said Manuel, 'you are incorrigible. When will you ever talk a word of sense?'

Angelo turned and stared into the flames for a time and glanced occasionally at me with a little smile on his lips. Then he said, 'I had a good upbringing. Andreas's grandmother, she was a strong woman and a good mother, a good Italian mother. Not like that tigress my brother has for a wife. It is my friends who have led me astray, that much is clear. As for you, Manuel Moreno, for a man who has lines from Lorca on the wall of his bar you are a strange one in my opinion. You have the mind of a poet but the soul of a machine.'

'The mind of a poet would be an interesting thing to have but the soul of a machine? I ask you, what sort of a mind do you have, Angelo Weissman?'

Angelo threw the end of the cigarette he had been smoking into the fire and turned in his chair to look at Manuel. Then he said, 'What I mean is that your understanding of things is that of a poet. You are intuitive, if letting your balls and your taste-buds govern your life can be called following your intuition. At any rate, it isn't logical. But when it comes down to the aesthetic issues, all you want is science. Look at you with your book of cocktails, all measured carefully, right

113

down to how many lumps of ice you are supposed to use. What's the point in that, I ask you. I remember when you refused to serve a guest a dry Martini because you only had Italian vermouth and no French . . .'

'But it's not the same.'

'And although she said to you, in a voice which the entire hotel could hear, that she didn't give a hedgehog's shit where the vermouth came from, you still told her she would have to have a sweet Martini or nothing. What sort of a soul do you have, I ask you. The soul of an old book, perhaps. A borrowed soul.'

'But Angelo, a dry Martini is a dry Martini.'

'Whether the vermouth is regular French or dry Italian?'

'You're a philistine. What do you know about cocktails.'

'I remember another saying I once heard, though where, I couldn't tell you: I trust no man. I used to trust my father until one day I saw him fuck my mother.'

'What has that got to do with it?'

'Nothing at all. But what has a book of someone else's cocktails got to do with things either if someone wants a drink and the barman won't serve it on principle? Let's face the reality of this, Manuel, you are a simple chemist and that's all there is to the matter.'

Manuel slapped the back of his right hand against the palm of his left and Angelo copied him and then, a few seconds later, I did the same and we all laughed. Then Angelo's face became serious.

'But this Bernard interests me. He is an artist, that much is clear. But what pain has driven him? Look at him, he is obsessed. How many cocktails must he have drunk to find his hundred and whatever recipes? I'll grant you, they're decent enough drinks. He knows what he's doing. But what grief or guilt brought him to it, I ask you that. Why this pseudonym?

114

Bernard, it's a good name, but what's wrong with a man's real name? And in any case, when someone is looking for perfection, the way he is, what sort of things is he trying to hide? This is my opinion. Bernard, he was a man with things to hide. Some English writer, I can't remember his name, he wrote that the love of perfection in an artist is to do with projecting guilt into the world of art. It's obvious, why else would you want your work to be perfect unless it's to make sure you give nothing of yourself away, unless it's a way of hiding the guilt which has driven you to your work. What do you know of this man, Manuel? You've drunk his cocktails, you've read his book, but what do you know of him?'

'I know him like I know my own brother. Bernard, he is my brother. He's my soul brother.'

'So your own brother must be an interesting man as well, but that's no answer. Do you know if Bernard had a brother? Do you know where he was born? Who he loved? What his fantasies were? If he was even a man?'

'Of course he was a man. And he was English, probably, or a Scot. His wife died when they had only been married for two weeks and he was very upset so he left the UK to travel around the whole world to look for a new girl for his life, so he spent a lot of time in cocktail bars looking for his new woman and he probably fucked a few whores along the way or something, and while he was at it he learnt a bit about cocktails. *Olé.*'

'And this from a man who calls the brother of his boss incorrigible. There is nothing that can be done for you, Manuel.'

But Angelo looked happy and suddenly he swung out his arm and held Manuel's head in an armlock and pretended to punch him in the face before he let him go, and we all laughed about it.

115

Angelo asked me, 'Is Hanna all right?'

'She's OK,' I said. 'A little nervous, I think, and not at all herself, but all right. When she comes back I shall take her to my room and put her to bed because she is tired.'

Angelo nodded and muttered something to himself which I could not hear but when I asked my uncle what he had said he waved away the question and then stood and went again to the bar where he refilled his glass and asked us if we wanted anything.

'Mix me a drink,' said Manuel. 'Any drink and from your own recipe. Make it up if you think you can do better than Bernie.'

I watched and wanted to laugh as Angelo scooped up some ice in a shaker and poured in some gin, shook it and strained it into a cocktail glass and then brought it over to Manuel.

'And the other thing,' he said, 'about this Bernard which interests me, he is a natural ironist. Of course his tongue is in his cheek when he says these things.' Angelo flicked through the book. 'Malibu Cocktail. This cocktail is named after the famous coast resort near Hollywood. It is very refreshing in hot weather. Or here. Hollywood Cocktail. This cocktail is very popular in America. Or this one.' He chuckled. 'Martini Special Cocktail. This makes a pleasant variation from the ordinary Martini cocktails. As if half the cocktails in this book aren't variations on Martini cocktails, I ask you. That's your trouble, Manuel. You take Bernard at his word. You take him too seriously. You don't realize that all alcoholics are life's natural ironists.'

Manuel sipped the drink Angelo had brought him and put it down and again slapped the back of his right hand against the palm of his left. Then he stood and went to the bar and poured in some spirits and liqueurs and mixers into the glass of gin, though I did not see which ones, apart from the

116

orange juice. When he came back he handed the glass to
Angelo who tasted it.

'This is better,' Angelo said. 'This is poetry. This is art.
You have taken the raw materials, or as raw as they come in
your line of business, and made something of them.'

'So I fooled you, I made a monkey out of you: this is a
Monkey Gland Cocktail. It's in the book. Gin, orange juice,
absinthe, grenadine, a twist of lemon. It's not to my taste on
a cold night like this, but you can't complain. Andreas, tell
me, I have the soul of a machine, your uncle thinks he's a
philosopher or poet or some such shit. How about you? What
sort of a soul have you got?'

I was quiet for a moment while I thought about the question. Then I told Manuel that I did not exactly know what
the soul should be. Manuel laughed and looked at Angelo,
but Angelo's face was stern. He walked to the windows at the
front of the lobby and stared out at the falling snow, then he
turned and looked at Manuel.

'The young people today, it's true, they don't know what
the soul is. And sometimes you have to ask yourself if they
even have a soul these days. What do I know, but if you ask
me we all lost something of our souls in recent years. As if
knowledge has ripped the very thing from our bodies. My
friend Saledin would argue that poetry was impossible after
the last war, after the Holocaust. Not so much because they
killed the Jews and others – people die, after all. But because
we know about it. If you think about it people didn't know
much about other people's troubles before the modern age.
And they had enough of their own to worry about. Nowadays
we all worry about everyone else's tragedies and we don't
have any of our own. What can you do about it, I ask you.
What can you do? Well, young people these days don't
understand much of anything as far as I can tell. Not much

by way of a soul, no sense of honour, no concept of what destiny might be. They might as well be dead already for all their lives are worth.'

Quite suddenly Alexandra came awake with a shout and Manuel put his arm around her shoulder and asked her what was wrong.

'Oh,' she said. 'I must have been dreaming. It was terrible.'

She hugged Manuel and then asked him for a sip of his drink. She wrinkled her nose when she tasted it and straightaway Angelo went behind the bar and poured a glass of gin for her and brought it over. She drank a large sip and then another and Angelo said, 'Find me a cocktail which would do as well for a woman who's had a bad dream.'

Manuel gestured at him and then they were silent for a time. I stared at the flames. A spark, a chip of burning wood, flew out of the fire and landed on the back of my hand. I watched it glowing, fading. I flicked the ash from my skin where the spark had left a tiny scar.

One day I could not find Elisa and I was worried about her. I looked for her in all the places she usually went to, but there was no sign of her so I went to Number Sixty-Nine. The Duchess did not know where she was either and asked some of the other whores to help us look. Finally I found her in Rafael's studio. He was working on a small glass figurine with his blowtorch. Elisa was reclining, nude, on the sofa by the window. When Rafael saw me he switched off his blowtorch and put it aside. 'But she is incredible, Andreas. It is five times now. This is the fifth work I have done with Elisa as my model. And she is a different person every time she works with me. It is incredible. To think that I have slept with her hundreds of times and never appreciated this. With Elisa I have a life's work ahead of me. I need never use another model.' Elisa said, 'I am very happy now, Andreas. Rafael is going to pay me the same as I would get working next door and he says at least three days a week. It's a lot. I think I can give up working for my mother.' She got up and came over to me and hugged me but she would not look me in the eye while she spoke. 'It's good, no? Of course we'll have a little less money. But I will have more free time and anyway it's better to do this work I think. It is less exhausting. And also I like to watch Rafael while he is working. It is so wonderful to watch an artist at work. Are you pleased for me, Andreas? Of course, the Duchess will be annoyed, I suppose, but I can take care of her OK. And, if you like, you can come to watch Rafael work as well. You would not mind that, Rafael, would you?'

Rafael said nothing, but motioned to Elisa to go back to her seat. He picked up the blowtorch and lit it again. 'Now I must concentrate because this is a difficult part. Andreas, sit over there, please.' He teased some molten glass away from the body of the figurine to make an arm but suddenly the whole sculpture seemed to explode and fell around Rafael in tiny slivers, burning his bare feet and arms. He quickly turned off the blowtorch and threw it to the floor and brushed the glass from his skin. Then he turned to me. 'Leave us. I cannot concentrate. If you had not been here this would not have happened.' I looked at Elisa but still she would not meet my eyes with hers. 'Go.' said Rafael.

It was quiet. There was only the sound of the wind and the crackling of the fire and the hum of the fluorescents and the fridges. Alexandra was sitting at the bar and reading the cocktail book. Manuel was looking out of the window. Angelo was staring into space. I thought I heard a noise from the kitchens.

'Ghosts,' said Angelo.

Manuel sighed and shook his head and Alexandra and I smiled at each other.

'Always at this time. They talk about the midnight hour, but that's bullshit. There are still too many people around at midnight.'

'Uschi swears she has seen them in the street. And she says they are always walking up the hill towards this place. She thinks they are the ghosts of inmates who died here. Oh, Andreas, can you imagine the trouble I used to have trying to get her to sleep at night?'

Alexandra got down from her stool and came and sat beside me.

'It makes me very nervous,' she said. 'I don't like it when

people talk about these things. Your great-grandfather, Rudolf, he would always sit with us when we were children and talk about ghosts and scare us all out of our wits. Ghosts and other things. Worse things. That's where Angelo gets it from, I should think. Rudolf, he used to say that before your family came to the village, before the sanatorium was built, the mountains used to come awake at night and walk about or something, though what he thought they were up to I'll never know. But when the sanatorium was built there was always someone awake at night, so the mountains stayed quiet and the people in the village could rest easy.'

Angelo broke in, 'He was an old idiot. It goes back to the beginning, when his own great-grandfather arrived here and . . .'

Just then there was a voice from the shadows behind Angelo. 'You are in my seat.'

Alexandra jumped and held my arm tightly but it was only the old man, Doctor Schnäpper.

'You know how I feel about it, Weissman,' he said. 'You know I find it distasteful to share my seat with others.'

Doctor Schnäpper stepped forward and Uncle Angelo sighed and stood up and turned to face him.

'What are you looking for, you old fool?' he asked.

'Looking for? What should I be looking for at this time of night? Perhaps you are unaware, but there is a storm raging outside my bedroom window. I can't sleep. It's no sin.'

He sat down in his armchair and Angelo took the seat on the other side of Alexandra. Manuel came over from the bar and asked Doctor Schnäpper if he wanted a drink.

'Please, Herr Moreno. A small Cognac if you will. Weissman, you were talking about your family again. That's the third time this week. And now I can see why.' He looked at me and nodded slowly. 'I knew something was up from the way your uncle has been moping around here for the last few days. And twice I've found him giving your girlfriend lessons in history, not that he knows anything about it. Hanna, is that her name? She's been moping around here nearly as much as he has.'

'Give it a break, Schnäpper. It's cold enough without any help from you.'

'Yes, it is cold. And the mountains are moving tonight. I've counted five major avalanches in the last four hours. Did you hear the last one? It was in the valley.' He shook his head. 'I hope that young couple, the foreigners, I hope they are far away tonight. Thank you, Herr Moreno. Your health, all of you.'

Very carefully, using both hands, he picked up the glass from the coffee table and sipped from it.

Alexandra said, 'Yes, they are in Rome for Easter week. Why? Do you think something might have happened to their house?'

Doctor Schnäpper laughed: 'I told them, but they wouldn't listen. They thought I was trying to put them off, but I told them. Within three years, I said, their house would be rubble. Well, it's rubble they'll be coming back to. They should have known better. He's a cold fish, but he's an intelligent man, the husband. He can ski; he should know there's no point in fighting the mountains. He should have understood why the village has grown up where it has. Does he think that the people who have lived here for so many centuries don't know where it's safe to build a house? Your friend, Weissman, the mountain man, Karl, he told them as well. Don't build it there, he said, build it here. But she, the wife, she kept going on about the view. Karl told her, obviously God did not intend the people who live here to be able to see into Switzerland from their front rooms or He would have made

123

the mountain a different shape. She wouldn't listen and now she'll learn more about God than the Pope can teach her in a week.'

'Well, for once I agree with you, Schnäpper. Although in my opinion it isn't a subject for discussion while the storm still has its ear pressed to the door. There's no point in tempting fate, after all.'

'In any case, I did not intend to interrupt your history lesson, Weissman. What were you saying about your ancestor?'

Angelo looked at Alexandra and back to Doctor Schnäpper. 'Nothing that can't keep.'

'Aha, then you must have been talking about the plague your family brought here. I'm surprised you don't know the story, Fräulein Schneider.'

'Of course I know the story, Doctor. Where do you think I've lived for the last forty years? Here. That's where.'

'I was about to explain to Alexandra that Rudolf's crazy ideas about mountains walking about at night came from his great-grandfather Heinrich, who, as you know, was a scientist and was able to tell people where they should and should not build their houses. For your information, Schnäpper, and you should know, it wasn't centuries of experience which taught the villagers that, but the good hypothetical method which my ancestor brought with him.'

'Amongst other things. The word on the street is that there wasn't much of a village left by the time your ancestor had been here long enough to build anything. The plague he brought with him from the East killed everyone.'

'Maybe so, but you won't deny that when he came here this village consisted of a church, a monastery and a bunch of shit-shovelling peasants who couldn't come to terms with the idea that God had it in for them.'

'I know all there is to know about Heinrich, Weissman.

124

You've no need to go on, as if I could give a damn. You're all a bunch of shit-shovelling peasants to this day, as far as I can tell. Metaphorically speaking.'

'There are still people whose blood turns to ice in their veins when they hear the words "German" and "Doctor" side by side, Schnäpper.'

'Quite so. And I'll grant you, Heinrich wasn't the idiot you might expect from looking at your brother. The sanatorium was a good building. If your brother hadn't torn it down it would have stood for another two hundred years. I'll give this place fifty before its walls have crumbled. There's frost damage on the north side already. I was looking at it only last week. And the incline of the roof is a disaster. The beams up there are warping and the slates are cracking. We'll need a new roof this summer. I'm in no doubt about that.'

'My brother's an arsehole, it has to be said.'

'It's what happens when a doctor starts thinking he's an architect.'

'You can talk.'

'So, the black sheep has returned to the fold.'

He stared at me and I sighed and got up and went to the reception desk where I could sit in peace. Schnäpper laughed and said loudly, 'Like uncle, like nephew, eh, Weissman?'

'Fuck off and die you old lizard. Leave the boy in peace.'

'There's little enough peace around here.'

'Then make the most of what peace there is.'

They fell silent.

After I had sat at the reception desk for a while I got bored and went back to join the others, but the fire was hot and then cold as the wind blew down the chimney and the smoke was getting in my eyes so I decided to move and went across to the reception desk again where I sat for a while longer. Alexandra was holding Manuel very close and I felt a little jealous of the warmth between them. Doctor Schnäpper and Angelo were staring at each other, still saying nothing. I decided to put on Angelo's anorak but I was still cold so after a while I told my uncle that I would go for a walk around the hotel to stretch my legs and make sure everything was OK.

I decided not to walk through the chalet complex and car parks as my uncle had done, but to patrol the corridors of the main building where there is heating. On the first floor there was nothing but on the second I heard music from one of the rooms. It was Thompson's room, I knew, and I stayed outside the door for a long time, listening, but I could hear nothing from inside except the sound of the radio playing and occasional creaks either from the bed or the floorboards, but

I could not tell which. Then I went to the third floor and then the fourth and the fifth and the sixth and finally right to the top, where the honeymoon suites and the private apartments of my family are. My own room, too. I sat on the floor outside my parents' apartment and smoked a cigarette and watched the security camera as it scanned the length of the corridor.

I noticed that the door to Doctor Schnäpper's room, opposite my parents' apartment, was ajar, so I got up and knocked gently on it. There was no answer so I pushed the door open and looked inside. I was quite surprised because there was hardly anything inside the room apart from the usual hotel furniture and there were not even any souvenirs or books or clothes. I looked down the corridor to make sure that no one was coming, then walked into the room and looked around. I thought about looking in the bathroom or in some cupboards, but then I heard the sound of the door at the end of the corridor opening and closing, so I quickly left the room. Doctor Schnäpper was coming towards me.

'Snooping?' he said.

I stuttered and said I was sorry. 'I noticed the door was open and there was no answer when I knocked. I was checking there was no one in there,' I said.

'A likely story. Anyway. Come on. Come on in.'

He walked past me into the room and held the door open and waved me in. Then he closed the door behind me and pointed to the armchair by the bed.

'Sit down. Make yourself comfortable. You're not Goldilocks. I couldn't give a sausage if you walk into my room uninvited. Why should I? There's nothing to see, as you can see. Sit. Make yourself comfortable. Would you like a schnapps? I have apricot or cherry. The apricot is good.'

He went into the bathroom and came back a moment later,

128

tightly holding a bottle and two small glasses which he put down on the floor at his feet when he sat down on the bed, quite close to me. I could smell his old skin and hair. It made me feel a bit sick but I smiled and took the glass he gave me.

'This is for sipping. I don't believe in drinking stuff you have to toss back. Drink this slowly. It's as good as Cognac.'

We toasted each other and I sipped the schnapps which was very good. Doctor Schnäpper studied my face closely and smiled and nodded when I took another small sip and toasted him again.

'It's good. From Austria. The real stuff.'

We said nothing for a few moments and then he asked me, 'And are you surprised that an old man should have so few possessions?'

I told him that I was a little and he laughed. 'So you should be. I made your father give me the room next door for a study. Everything's in there. But I like this room as it is now. Nothing to distract me while I'm in here.'

'It's like my room,' I said. 'My father threw out all my stuff, so I have nothing now.'

'I wouldn't complain, if I were you. The more things you have the more space you need, and the more space you have the more things you get. It has to end somewhere, so either you become a fascist or a Buddhist. One way or another it screws you up.'

He stared at me for a while and I looked away.

'Like uncle like nephew,' he said. 'I remember him at your age. Just before he ran away for the last time. He could hardly look me in the eye either. Illness does that to people. It was no surprise to me when your father pulled down the old place. He never did have the stomach for it.'

He spread his arms and looked from one hand to the other. 'These hands.'

He shook his head and then looked at me closely again.

'It's not catching. It's genetic, they say. I'm a freak of nature, if you like. And it has its funny side. Yogic masters practise shutting down their senses for years in preparation for entering heaven. For some of us it comes naturally. I remember when it started. Just a tingling in my fingers and toes. Now it's along to my elbows and halfway up my shins. I made these splints myself. Can't feel a thing. It'll get worse if I live long enough. Progressive Neurological Disorder. That's what they call it. I told them, when it comes down to it, life's a Progressive Neurological Disorder. Told me to shut up and do my exercises.'

He stared at me again and I looked away again and he laughed and shook his head.

'Your girlfriend's downstairs. The harlot's daughter. She seemed agitated but she wasn't going to talk about it. Her mother's with her, but I'd get back to her if I were you. She's on the edge, that one. Off you go.'

I knocked back my drink and Doctor Schnäpper opened the door for me. As I passed him he grabbed hold of my arm and held me tightly and I stopped and we looked at each other. He nodded and smiled.

'You can't catch it. It's genetic. That's all.'

He nodded again and I pulled free of him and walked away without looking back.

W hen I got to the lobby Hanna was sitting at the bar with her mother. I joined them and asked where Thompson and Nichol were and Hanna said that Thompson was in Nichol's room talking to him, but that he would be coming down soon and then we would all have some food together. Manuel came over to the bar and opened up the jukebox and asked Alexandra what would she like to hear.

'Play "Lonely Night",' she said. 'It's good for this weather and the time.'

Manuel chose the song and Alexandra started to sing along with it and Hanna joined in as well. Just then, Thompson came through the doors and Hanna stopped singing and moved away from me a little. Alexandra stood up and waltzed into the middle of the lobby and swayed and ran her hands up and down her body while she sang. When she finished we all clapped and I cheered and whistled and Alexandra bowed.

'I didn't realize you were so talented,' said Thompson. 'You can sing.'

Alexandra hit him on the arm, but quite gently. 'Of course

I can sing,' she said. 'I am a singer, or I was. But Hanna is better than I am. And she can play the piano very well as well.'

'You should give us a bit of a concert. What do you say, Manuel? Get the girls to sing for us in a bit? I think we ought to have a bite to eat first, though, because I don't know about you bunch of comedians, but I'm bloody hungry.'

Manuel did not answer Thompson, but he slapped Angelo on the back and said, 'Hey, mate, we're keeping you awake tonight. You haven't seen so much excitement since the soldiers were here two years ago.'

Alexandra giggled and Thompson looked at her. She went red and said, 'Nothing, nothing, it's nothing.'

'Go on, what happened then?'

'Some soldiers from Switzerland, they were lost and the weather was lousy so they came to the hotel. I don't think I've ever served so many drinks in one night here. Alexandra, she kept them entertained.'

'What, all of them?'

'Manuel, you are terrible. No, no, I did not entertain them in the way you think. But they wanted a – how is it? – a floor show. I quite enjoyed it, in fact. I have never done something like this before and we had a good time.'

Angelo said: 'If you call that a good time. Nearly every guest in the hotel wanted to leave the next day. Well, if it's to your taste, I suppose, but personally I have a different idea of what a good time might be.'

'Yeah, so what's your idea of a good time then, night porter? Sitting here all night staring at the walls?'

'No. But, for example, I recall when I was staying in Madrid with my friend Eduardo. We were working each night until dawn and when we returned to the apartment it was our habit to sit on the balcony with a beer before we

132

went to sleep. There is nothing like a beer after a long night's work for a start, but the point was that in the apartment on the opposite side of the street there was a woman, a young woman who it seemed lived alone which was unusual in those days in Spain. Every morning while we were sitting there she would come out on to her balcony to drink a coffee and she was always naked. She knew we were there – I am sure of that because once I bumped into her in the street and she blushed and ran away – but as long as she could pretend she didn't see us, she didn't care about it. Well, that was a good time. Every morning to see such a vision. We would sleep well and the thought of it keeps you going at night when you just want to get to bed and nothing more. You can spend much of your life waiting for moments like that, enjoying them, remembering them.'

'Well, mate, if I was you I'd have been over there like a shot.'

'No, you do not understand. What is the point? She was probably very stupid and it was better to imagine what she might be like in the ideal world than to find out the reality of the matter. Manuel, will you fill my glass?'

'I reckon it's time you made me another cocktail, Manuel, and Alex and Hanna can go and find us something to eat.'

I said that I would go and help them and Hanna asked if Nichol would be eating as well.

'No, the boring git's gone to sleep. Can't take it, can he.'

In the kitchens I used my keys to unlock all the fridges and cupboards and Alexandra and Hanna searched through them and took out the things they wanted. I sat on a surface and watched them while they worked, but none of us said much apart from Alexandra who told Hanna what to do. The wind had grown stronger and there was a loud noise outside which made Hanna jump and she nearly cut herself with the knife she was using. I told her it was just snow falling from the roof and then I went to the delivery entrance and opened the door so I could look outside. There was nothing to see except snow, though, so I closed it again. While they prepared the food I made myself a coffee and drank it quickly. Then Thompson came in and walked around the kitchen looking at things. He picked up a fig from a bowl of fresh fruit and peeled it and broke it into two parts. He went over to Hanna and told her to close her eyes and open her mouth. She did and Thompson put half of the fig in her mouth, told her to keep her eyes closed and quickly left. Hanna chewed the fruit and swallowed and said, 'Jonny?'

Alexandra told her that he had gone and Hanna smiled and shrugged. Then I took a filleting knife from one of the knife-racks. I ran my finger along it but it was not very sharp, so I took a steel from the rack and sharpened the knife carefully. I wiped the blade on a towel and ran it along my thumb and this time it cut into my skin and a moment later some blood started to flow from the wound. I watched the blood collect on my thumb and then break the surface tension which held it there. A few spots fell on the floor and I wiped my boot over them and sucked my thumb clean before I put the knife back in its place.

'But you are terrible.' Hanna was staring at me. 'Don't you know about kitchens? Give me the knife, I'll clean it. But you are crazy. For four years you have worked in kitchens and still you do this. I will not eat your food again.'

I handed her the knife and she washed it and put it back on the rack. She shook her head and said, 'You are a dangerous person to have around. Go on. Go back and join the others. We don't need your blood here.'

When I got back to the lobby I put some more logs on the fire and sat down and watched Manuel show Thompson how to mix a drink.

Before very long, Hanna and Alexandra brought the food through. They had cooked escalopes of veal and made some potato salad and some green salad. They brought it all in on a trolley and I helped them put the plates out on the coffee table by the fire.

'We can eat here, no?' said Alexandra. 'It's warmer by the fire.'

As we were sitting down to eat, my father appeared as if from nowhere. Manuel stood up but my father waved him back into his seat and reached out to shake Thompson's hand.

'I am Doctor Wiessman,' he said. 'The manager of the hotel.'

'Thompson. How do you do, mate?'

'Very well, thank you. Are my staff performing adequately?'

Thompson carried on eating and spoke with his mouth

full: 'More than adequately, Doc. Wish I could get such good staff down my way. Difficult to find.'

'Good staff is difficult to find, it is true. In former times it was different.'

'Is the chopper going to be flying in the morning or what? Only I've got a business meeting in Venice and it's important.'

'I regret, if the weather remains this way it will be impossible to leave the village. I believe that it is a geographical problem. But the hotel will pay for your room, if you have to remain at our pleasure for any extra nights. And meals and drinks, of course. It is the least we can do.'

'And the most, more like. If I'd known I was going to be stuck here I'd never bloody come.'

My father nodded and smiled. He said to Angelo, 'Have you done your work?'

Angelo did not look up but said, 'There are beers, there is food, there are women. This too can be work,' and Thompson laughed.

My father frowned and turned to look at me. 'Andreas.'

I followed my father to the reception desk and he called to Manuel, 'Herr Moreno, two calvados. With ice.' Manuel jumped up and went to the bar and brought us the drinks.

'I hope my brother has been showing you the ropes,' said my father. 'He is not a bad brother, but he is an unreliable worker. Are you tired? If you grow tired you may go to bed. It is better if you take things easy these first few days. Until you become accustomed to the hours, and then you can assume your full responsibilities.'

He toasted me and drank his calvados in one and I did the same. Then he looked at me closely.

'Yes, you are a young man already. I am sorry I have not seen you much before. Tomorrow, perhaps, I will have time to speak with you at length. Your mother, she worried about you while you were in the military, do you know that? She didn't want you to go and said that we should use the loophole so you would gain exemption. But I told her that it was a good thing for a boy to do at your age. To learn some discipline. From discipline you learn self-discipline, and then you can do things. It teaches you something about life and when you return you are a man already. A young man, perhaps, but more than a boy. If your uncle had done his military service things might be different. You will come to notice that.'

He nodded to the others on his way out and I went back to my seat by the fire.

'More bullshit?' asked Angelo and I nodded. Angelo said to Thompson, 'Back from his military service for less than a week and already his father starts on him, even though he hasn't even made the effort to welcome the boy home with a meal or anything at all. He might be my brother, but he's an arsehole in most respects. He's the sort of man who takes a cold shower and then rubs himself down with snow, and all that before he even gets out of bed. I don't know what his wife thinks about it. Him and the Lizard, they're made for each other.'

Thompson asked who or what the lizard was and Angelo grunted and nudged Manuel.

'The Lizard, that's Manuel's name for him,' he said. 'He used to work at the sanatorium when it was still here. Doctor Schnäpper.' Angelo laughed. ' "Doctor" is good. He was a doctor. A surgeon. Though I shudder to think what sort of surgery a German of his age might have done. He's got something wrong with him. Since he was young the nerves in his hands have been playing tricks on him so he had to give it all up and come here to plague us with his nonsense. He was an administrator, responsible for the building. He's full of shit. He lives on the top floor because he wouldn't leave when the old place got pulled down. He's an old bastard. He sits here by the fire all day staring at you and creeps around the hotel at night. You just missed him earlier. The Snake would be a better name for the poisonous old fool.'

'Although he tells some good tales about the old days.'

'Tales, yes, but that's all they are, You see, Mr Thompson, all these people who came here to cough their guts out, the Lizard, he met a few of them. He likes to think he taught them a thing or two, as well, but as I remember people couldn't get away from him fast enough. If you can put up with that sort of thing he's entertaining enough, I suppose, but I've never had the stomach for it myself. And his mother was American, which hardly helps.'

Thompson said, 'Yeah, I can't stand Yanks. My old man was a Yank. The bastard raped my mother and her old man made him marry her. He had an accident a few years ago. Died.'

Angelo finished eating and then pulled a head of garlic from his jacket and broke it into cloves. Then he peeled them and sliced some of them. I reached over and took a couple of slices and so did Alexandra. Angelo motioned to Thompson.

'Try some,' he said. 'It's good for you, for the circulation, and it goes well with the drink when you've already eaten. Aside from that there's a certain intimacy in eating garlic with someone. It helps you get to know them better.'

Thompson took a slice and chewed on it for a moment and Manuel said, 'You people gotta lot of problems, you know that.'

Angelo shrugged. 'Well, you have to seek God in your own way.'

After that everyone was quiet for a while and Thompson

140

helped himself to some more garlic and then took another helping of salad. Angelo said to him, 'Of course, if you've been to the Alhambra you must know the black bees which live in the gardens of the Generalife . . .'

Manuel broke in, 'Everywhere in the South, I've told you before, Angelo.'

'In any case, one finds them in the Generalife. Great black creatures which settle on flowers only half their size. My friend, Saledin – perhaps I have mentioned him to you – he would always say that they were the houris of the garden. It's an interesting thought. And the black cats, he would say that they might be the lost souls of the architects of the palace, doomed to wander in its gardens until the day of judgement. He was being whimsical, of course. I remember one time in the Generalife, in the gardens as we were sitting there sharing some cake and drinking wine – wine, I always said to him; God is merciful, he always answered – and a black bee nearly landed on me and I panicked trying to get away from it. Don't worry, he said, she can see you're no flower. And I asked him how he worked that out. Maybe she was about to stick her tongue in my ear. It happens. Houris, he said, not whores, you infidel. You infidel, that was good. Well, as I say, you have to seek God in your own way.'

Thompson took a final mouthful and threw down his fork and knife and belched. He stared at Angelo with no expression and then said, 'That was good, that. You cook that, Alex, did you? No offence, Hanna, but it's got a mother's touch. Plates could have been hotter. There's nothing I hate more than cold plates. But apart from that, not a bad job at all. Which is more than I can say for Manuel's effort. Manuel, this is fucking disgusting. Do you know, Alex, I took one look at this bloke and I thought: quality material here. But you can be wrong and I'm beginning to wonder if I was.

This is going to make me puke, so get me a beer, will you. Do excuse me, I've got to have a slash.'

When he had gone, Manuel stayed where he was. His face had gone red and Alexandra squeezed his arm and told him not to worry. When Thompson came back he looked at Manuel and asked where his beer was. Manuel did not move but carried on eating and then Thompson picked up his glass and threw it quite hard against the wall and showered everyone with the cocktail, though the glass did not break.

'Strong glasses, Mr Thompson,' said Manuel.

'Or soft walls, more like. Get me a fucking beer. Now.'

'Get it yourself. I'm eating.'

Thompson grabbed Manuel by the arm and pulled him out of the chair and Manuel swung his fist at him, hitting him on the side of the head. The rest of us stood and backed away from the table, but Thompson held up his hands.

'All right, you crazy spic,' he said. 'I'll get it myself.'

Thompson went to the bar and got a beer and sat there drinking it. Manuel carried on eating as if nothing had happened. After a short time Thompson left the lobby. Angelo said, 'See how God has blessed my nephew. See how Andreas has felt the hot blast of His breath. Andreas, your face is red. Go and see where our guest has gone.'

He motioned to me to go to the reception desk and see where Thompson went by watching the security cameras, so I did and I watched as Thompson went up the stairs to the third floor which was where Nichol's room was. He knocked on the door for a long time before Nichol answered and then he went in. I told Angelo what was happening and he turned to Manuel and looked at him thoughtfully for a moment.

'Manuel, it might be best if you left for a time. Until he calms down. We don't need this trouble in the middle of the night, with fighting and what do I know.'

Manuel nodded and left straightaway, after saying that he was tired in any case. I watched on the monitors as he went into the room on the first floor he had used earlier. Angelo sighed loudly.

'Always something like this. Whenever there are people in the night there is trouble. Take my advice, Andreas, don't encourage it. If people want a drink give them a drink and be civil, but never encourage them.'

Alexandra came over to the reception desk and stood close to me and looked over my shoulder at the monitors.

'And what are Hanna and I going to do now,' she said. 'All our men have gone and there are only the ghosts.'

She pretended to shiver and rested her chin on my shoulder. I turned round and smiled at her and walked across to the fire and crouched in front of it. Then Thompson came back on his own.

'Where's Manuel?'

'He has gone to bed, Mr Thompson.'

'Well what did he do that for? He's not still upset about our little contretemps, is he? Silly bugger. I can't help it, you know. I'm always doing that sort of thing, getting into bloody silly fights about nothing. If he wasn't a mate I'd have beaten the shit out of him. So, Alex, why don't you give us a song, then? Hanna and the kid can clear up and you can entertain me and the night porter here, because that's what this place needs, if you ask me, a bit of entertainment. It needs a bit of action, if you want to know what I think. I mean, look at us: we've got booze, we've got music, we've got girls – not enough girls, but still – but we haven't got any action. I don't know how you people do it, sitting on your arses up here in the middle of bloody nowhere with diddly bloody nothing to do. I'd go bloody mad, I would . . .'

Hanna and I cleared the table and I pushed the trolley out

while my uncle chose a song and Alexandra started to sing. We could hear her from the kitchens while we stacked the dishes in the dishwasher and Hanna started to sing along quietly as well. Then I sat down and smoked a cigarette while Hanna cleared up the mess which she and her mother had made earlier. While she was doing that I noticed that she had a bruise on her shoulder and her dress was slightly ripped. I asked her how it happened.

'It's nothing. Jonny, he got a little bit excited, you know.'

'Did he hurt you?' I asked and she shook her head but said nothing.

When she had finished clearing up she asked me if I wanted to go outside with her. I wanted some fresh air as well so I said yes and unlocked the delivery entrance. Outside the snow was deep because it had drifted but it was quite easy to tread down and reach the roadway which Hans had cleared earlier on.

'Shit,' said Hanna. 'Maybe this isn't such a good idea.'

I asked her if she wanted to go back in but she said no. 'Let's walk round to the front. We can surprise them.'

The snow was not falling as strongly as it had been and I could see the shadow of the treeline a few metres above us. I picked up a handful of snow and rolled it into a ball and threw it as far as I could. Hanna took hold of my arm and we slid and stumbled down to the road. Then she stopped and I stopped too and turned to face her. She was shivering and her teeth were chattering.

'We should go inside,' I said. 'You're cold.'

'No, I'm all right. It's good. I want to be cold. I want to freeze.'

Suddenly she threw her arms round me and held me quite tightly so I put my arms round her and hugged her too. Then she let go and took a step back and stared at me. We

144

were beside the windows of the dining hall and from inside there was a little light. Her face was pale and her lips looked blue. Snow was settling on her hair and in the folds of her dress, but she had stopped shivering. She seemed calm.

'Come on,' I said, but she did not move. 'Come on,' I said again. 'You're going to die.'

'Yes. Let's go back. It's better if we go back through the kitchen. Jonny, he's nervous of you. He wasn't pleased when he saw us sitting together earlier.'

Just as she spoke there was the crackle and crunch of snow sliding over ice. It was close by and Hanna and I froze where we were. The noise grew louder until it was a roar and suddenly to the side of us, at the reach of our vision, snow crashed into the trees and there was the sound of wood splintering as the avalanche exhausted itself. Then quiet again. Hanna was shaking.

'It's OK,' I said. I hugged her but she broke free. 'It was just a baby,' I said. 'From the ravine. It happens every year. We're OK here.'

She turned and made her way back to the kitchens and I followed her a few paces behind.

After I told Elisa that I would be going back to the village she went to stay at Number Sixty-Nine. 'It's no good,' she said. 'I will die if I stay here with you and know that you are leaving. I will die inside myself.' I spent the next day saying goodbye to people I had got to know and getting rid of stuff which I had bought since I arrived in Como but did not want to take with me. On my last night I did not sleep, but sat alone on the balcony of Elisa's apartment, drinking whisky and smoking some hashish my captain had brought earlier in the week. When it was light I packed and got my things ready to take back to the barracks. I heard the sirens in the street, the shouting, but I was too busy to see what was going on. When I got outside I found that my way along the Via C— was blocked by policemen and a big crowd of people. No one seemed to know what the trouble was, but then I recognised Rafael sitting by the roadside, his head bowed, his arms crossed. His hair was burnt away and his face was blackened with soot and streaked with tears and he smelt of smoke. I asked him what was up. He stared at me as if he had never seen me before. 'My sculptures,' he said. 'My life's work. All of it.' I asked him what had happened. 'Fire. It spread like wildfire. I could save nothing. All of them, dead. Ashes.' Then he uncrossed his arms and held his hands close to my face. They were blistered and raw. Where his fingers had been there were only charred stumps.

I tried to make my way through the crowd to the police barrier to call an ambulance for Rafael. Ahead, a siren sounded quickly and the people moved aside to let a police car past. She was sitting in the back staring straight ahead, smiling and calm. I shouted to her, Elisa, Elisa, but if she heard me she did not show it. I pushed past some people and hammered on the window of the car with my fist. She did not turn to look. The policeman driving shouted at me and when I hammered on the window again he drew his gun and waved it at me. I backed away and followed the car until it reached the edge of the crowd and sped off, its siren wailing.

When we got back to the lobby Angelo was standing by the window looking out.

'That was the ravine, by the sound of it,' he said.

I nodded but did not tell him that we had been outside. Thompson and Alexandra were at the bar. Thompson asked Hanna, 'Can you sing as well as your mother, then? Because I was just saying to her that when I open my new bar down in Malaga I'm going to be looking for a regular singer and I reckon Alex fits the bill. You could come too, if you like. Good money in it and top clients. You could probably earn yourself a bit extra on the side, as long as you kept quiet about it. Can't let a place like that get a bad name, after all. What do you think?'

Hanna looked at Alexandra who shrugged and Hanna shrugged too.

'Well, please yourself. Jesus, if I was you I'd jump at the chance to get out of this shithole. Do you know if the helicopter's going to be flying in the morning yet? What time is it? Night porter, do me a favour, put a call through to my man Mace again, will you. I'll have to let him know I might not make this meeting tomorrow.'

Angelo told him that the telephone was dead.

'You what? It can't be. Telephones don't bloody go dead in this day and age. You are joking, I hope.'

'I am very sorry, Mr Thompson. Perhaps an avalanche, or the wind. I don't know.'

'This is brilliant, this is. Stuck in a shithole hotel in the middle of bloody nowhere with a bunch of amateurs who couldn't organise a piss-up in Torremolinos and the bloody phones don't work. This is just what I need. Do you realize how important this meeting I have tomorrow is? Don't you get it? We're talking millions of dollars down the drain if I can't get there. And I've got a tender to put in the next day in Zurich which is worth even more. Midday, if I'm not there with that document, I'm ruined. Haven't you got a telex or a fax or anything?'

'Of course we have a fax, but the telephones are not working. It is not possible to send a fax if the telephone is not working, you understand.'

'What about a radio telephone or something?'

'At the mountain rescue station, yes, but it is very difficult to reach when the weather is this way. Even Andreas would not try it and he is one of the best skiers in the village.'

Thompson looked at me.

'Is that true,' he asked.

I said that yes, it was true and that anyone would have to be crazy to try to reach the station even in daylight with the snow and the wind as strong as it was.

'What if it clears tomorrow?'

'Then it is possible, yes.'

Thompson turned and looked at the window where the snow had banked up to nearly head-height.

'All right, then, tomorrow. If the weather's better. You can take me there.'

Angelo looked at me and frowned when he saw that I was

about to speak so I closed my mouth again. I was not in the mood to argue about it, anyway. Thompson put his hand against the window and ran his fingertips down it.

Angelo sighed and said to me, 'I've had enough of this, Andreas. I'm going to my room. There are better things to do. You can stay here or go to bed. It's up to you. I don't care. No one will miss us.'

He went to the door and checked that it was locked. Then he went over to the fireplace and put the guard in front of the fire. He kissed Alexandra on the cheek and then Hanna and then he was gone.

Thompson stayed by the window for a while and then started walking around the lobby, slapping his hand against his leg as he went. He came over to me and stood looking at me. He sniffed.

'I fucking hate this place. It's worse than fucking Morocco.' He walked to the door and pushed against it. 'Can't even get out of the fucking hotel.'

I moved towards him and jangled my keys but without turning he shouted, 'Piss off!' He walked in a wide circle and pushed against the door again, took a few paces back, then ran towards it, dropping his shoulder before he hit it. The door did not give but the security alarm started to ring behind the reception desk. Thompson's face was red and he bared his teeth. He ran over to the bar and picked up one of the stools by its legs, swung it around his head and smashed it into the plate-glass window where he had been standing before. The stool seemed to bounce off the glass with no effect and he swung it, hammering it into the glass again and again until the effort had exhausted him and he threw the stool aside and fell to his knees. He looked up at the window, stared at it. I followed his gaze. A crack had appeared in the centre of the glass. It was small at first but slowly it was growing in length.

Thompson got to his feet and watched as the crack crept out-
wards, forking at either end, forking again and again until the
one crack had become a web of fissures. Suddenly the whole
window seemed to shiver and with a great snap and crash the
glass fell into fragments at Thompson's feet and the snow
which had drifted against the window flowed into the lobby
followed by flurries of snowflakes and the cold mountain air.
Thompson climbed up into the empty window-frame. He
shouted something but his words were lost in the wind and
the ringing of the alarm. He turned and looked at me, then at
Hanna and Alexandra. His expression was triumphant. He
jumped down and went behind the bar. He took a bottle of
champagne and crossed to where Alexandra was standing
with Hanna, kissed Hanna on the cheek and whispered in
Alexandra's ear. Alexandra nodded and then he went to the
lift and called it. Hanna said, 'But why?'

'Like I told your mother, if Manuel's gone to bed, I might as
well give her a whirl. She can show me what she's made of. It's
no reflection on you, Hanna. Variety, that's all. Spice of life.'

Alexandra took Hanna's arm and led her to the fireside and
sat her down and spoke to her. A moment later Thompson
came over to me and said, 'You're a good man. Look after
her for us, mate. She's a good kid. Here.'

He took a wad of money from his wallet and handed it to
me. I took it and put it in my pocket without counting how
much he had given me. It seemed like a lot. Thompson went
back to the lift.

'She's a good kid, mate,' he said. 'Why don't you make the
most of it. Have one on me.'

Alexandra joined him and they entered the lift. The doors
closed behind them and the gears droned and crunched and
they were gone.

A ngelo came running through the stairway doors, breathless and flustered.

'What is it?' he asked. 'A fire?'

I pointed at the pile of snow and shattered glass and the empty window-frame. His beeper was still going and he seemed suddenly to notice it again. He went behind the reception desk and used his key to switch off the alarm.

'Thompson?'

I nodded.

'He'll pay for it. It's no problem. But we should board the hole.'

'No!'

Hanna stood and took a few steps towards us.

'Leave it now,' she said. 'It's right. It's the way it should be. Please.'

Angelo muttered to himself and kicked some of the snow and glass around. He turned to me and shrugged.

'When you're on your own you'll see. It's different. The quiet. It sharpens your senses. You hear things which can't be heard otherwise. See things too. It's alarming. Disquieting.

151

You get used to it.'

He shook his head and glanced at the window-frame, looked around the lobby, turned and slowly made his way towards the stairway doors and then he was gone.

When the echoing of his footsteps on the stairs had finished, Hanna went back to the fireside. I sat at the reception desk for a while and smoked a cigarette and tried to keep warm. The wind was dropping, the snow falling only lightly now. When I looked again at Hanna she was asleep, her mouth open. An avalanche in the valley disturbed her and she shifted and moved her legs apart so that her dress rode up revealing bruised thighs and hair which glistened under the fluorescents. Everything was quiet. I looked around the lobby, at the snow and broken glass. There were things to clear up but I decided to leave them as they were. 'No, don't clear the table,' Elisa would say. 'Leave everything as it is, then in the morning we will remember what a time we had.'

I got up and went over to Hanna and lifted her in my arms and carried her to the lift and up to the seventh floor, along the corridor and into my room. I put her down on the bed and then kicked some of the snow out of the room, on to the balcony, and I closed the french windows, but not the curtains. I took off Hanna's dress and lightly brushed my fingers against her skin where it was blue and black and red and gently kissed her throat. Then I took off my own clothes and sat on the sofa drinking whisky straight from the bottle and smoking a cigarette. I got up and switched off the light and sat down again. Hanna stirred a little on the bed. Her skin was goose-bumped. She stirred again and mumbled something, but I could not understand what she said. I did not want to move her again in case I woke her, so I took a blanket from the bottom of the wardrobe and spread it over her, then lay down on the sofa. It was cold and I shivered. 'As if

God has reached out and touched you,' Elisa would say. 'As if He has drawn a finger from the base of your spine to the nape of your neck.'

I stubbed the cigarette out in the tumbler I had been using earlier and looked down at my skin which was pale and shining in the half-light as the fragility of the night began to give way to the cold certainty of another day.

Abacus now offers an exciting range of quality titles by both established and new authors. All of the books in this series are available from:
    Sphere Books,
    P.O. Box 11,
    Falmouth,
    Cornwall TR10 9EN.

Alternatively you may fax your order to the above address. Fax No. 0326 76423.

Payments can be made as follows: Cheque, postal order (payable to Macdonald & Co (Publishers) Ltd) or by credit cards, Visa/Access. Do not send cash or currency. UK customers: please send a cheque or postal order (no currency) and allow 80p for postage and packing for the first book plus 20p for each additional book up to a maximum charge of £2.00.

B.F.P.O. customers please allow 80p for the first book plus 20p for each additional book.

Overseas customers including Ireland, please allow £1.50 for postage and packing for the first book, £1.00 for the second book, and 30p for each additional book.

NAME (Block Letters) ....

ADDRESS..

....

☐ I enclose my remittance for _____

☐ I wish to pay by Access/Visa Card

Number ☐☐☐☐☐☐☐☐☐☐☐☐☐☐☐☐☐

Card Expiry Date ☐☐☐☐